Sourdough and Cyanide

A Laughing Loaf Bakery Mystery

Book 4

Victoria Kazarian

With love, to my sisters,
Pam and Kerry

Chapter One

Tuesday, December 3

That morning at 7 a.m., I flipped the sign on the front door of The Laughing Loaf Bakery to OPEN. When I unlocked and opened the door a gush of cool, wet air hit me in the face.

It was the beginning of December. Rain, cold, dampness everywhere.

Winter—Santa Cruz mountain style—was here.

I had three days to prep my assistant, Beck, to take over for me. I was leaving my bakery in someone else's hands for the very first time. So I could head up to California wine country with a man who made me weak in the knees.

I sighed as I set today's joke of the day on its stand. I was almost ashamed of myself for putting this one out. A dad joke so bad, almost any dad would boo it.

Laughing Loaf Joke of the Day
The other day I saw a baguette in a cage.
It was bread in captivity.

When the usual group of high schoolers came into the bakery at 7 a.m., stopping off on their way to River Grove High School, they groaned.

"Oh, my God, Gracie," Skyler Robbins, River Grove High School's senior class clown, said, after he gave me his order for a cappuccino. "Are you getting low on jokes? That's awful."

I was in a really good mood this morning. I smiled back at him cheerfully. "I knew that would get a *rise* out of you."

Groans spread through the line, along with cries of "Make her stop!"

Sky leaned over the counter toward me, a sober expression on his face. "Gracie, I'll give you that one," he said in a lowered voice. "That was a pretty good comeback. But I have a reputation to uphold, so I'm not going to laugh at it."

"Fair enough, Sky." I chuckled to myself as I headed to the display case to plate his usual cinnamon roll.

Within ten minutes, the teenagers had their coffee, cinnamon rolls, and French toast sticks, and had settled in at the dining area tables to finish up studying before taking off for school at 8:15 a.m.

Since it was finals week, they pulled binders and textbooks out of their backpacks right away and got to work. The room smelled like coffee, cinnamon, and damp flannel shirts. Beck and I looked at each other and smiled, savoring the quiet.

"Don't you love mornings like this?" Beck sighed.

After an hour, the teenagers shoved their books back into their backpacks and pulled on jackets in a flurry of activity. The bakery quickly emptied out. Rain beat down on the bakery awning in front, and I couldn't see anyone else out on the street, which was probably smart.

This could be a slow morning.

"Can you make me an oat milk latte, Beck?"

"Of course!" Beck said cheerfully, returning to the espresso machine. "Any pumpkin spice in that?"

"Do you even need to ask?"

Beck gave me a thumbs up and got to work.

One thing was missing today: my little dog, Biga. At 4:30 a.m., when we were supposed to leave to go to the bakery, Biga sniffed and looked around. *Freezing rain? I'll stay in bed, thanks.*

In a few minutes, our adult regulars began tromping in from the rain, setting their umbrellas in the stand, and shaking themselves off on the mat before they got in line to order. Since most customers this morning chose to stay inside, the murmur of conversation in the dining room gradually built to a low roar.

This was my happy place: a warm, cozy bakery full of customers shooting the breeze with each other and starting the day at a nice slow pace.

As I brought a tray of warm orange-cranberry scones out of the back room, I thought about the instructions I'd give Beck during her test run for closing today. This week she was getting practice opening the bakery, closing up, and setting up for the following days' bakes.

I had no doubt Beck could handle it, though when I first brought up the idea, she'd looked terrified at the thought. The practice was mostly so she'd feel confident running the bakery by herself.

I was The Laughing Loaf's founder and its only bread maker. Because of that, I'd put myself in a situation where it was hard for me to take time off. So, I decided that bread would also take a vacation during my getaway. We would sell only pastries, scones, and rolls for the three days—things

Beck excelled at. We'd edge toward Christmas on a sweet note.

Beck came up with the name: Winter Pastry Fest.

Beck was talented and loyal, and hiring her had been one of the best decisions I'd ever made. Recently I'd given her an education fund and the promise of time off to take classes in her pastry specialty.

After a scary October, when Russian agents came after me looking for tech secrets my ex-husband had left behind, Thanksgiving had come and gone in a flurry at The Laughing Loaf Bakery.

The week before Thanksgiving, customers pre-ordered baked goods for holiday gatherings. It was an incredible amount of work for Beck and me. We filled the orders with the help of two students I hired part-time—Chloe Westerman, granddaughter of River Grove Police Chief Dave Westerman, and Chloe's good friend, Aiden Franzi. Then late the day before Thanksgiving, I wearily hung up the CLOSED sign on the bakery door and went home to prepare for a small Thanksgiving feast with my professor father, his lady friend, Mary Jo Hartman, and my boyfriend, Nate Behrens.

I had never baked so much in my life.

So, you can see why I was looking forward to this coming Friday. Nate and I would leave on our getaway to Sonoma County, a wine and culinary hotspot north of the Golden Gate Bridge.

Beck had come up with a very ambitious plan for her three days in charge. When we hit our mid-morning lull at The Laughing Loaf, Beck handed me her final draft of the Winter Pastry Fest menu. I set aside the tub of brioche dough I'd just mixed, and the two of us stood over the metal bread table to go over the menu and ingredient list.

Cinnamon rolls
Cranberry orange scones
White chocolate cherry scones
Beignets
Peppermint beignets
Dark chocolate beignets
Apple tarts
Pumpkin raisin bread

"So you've got some regular items and some variations on what we make—which is smart. I know you've tested this, but it's a lot. You're okay with taking all this on?"

Beck nodded confidently. "You've taught me how important it is to prep. So I'll have the scones rolled, laminated, and cut on trays in the freezer, like you do, Gracie. Ready to bake. The beignet dough will be chilling in the fridge as usual—I'll mix it up early, and Chloe can help me fry them up in the mornings. She's willing to come in as early as I need her to. After they helped out for Thanksgiving week, Chloe and Aiden have the espresso machine down. We've got this."

I studied her young face, glowing with excitement at the opportunity. Beck had come a long way in the past year-and-a-half of working at the bakery. When I'd hired her, she'd been only 22, homeschooled through high school with her five brothers, and her only job experience had been babysitting and working at a day care. She'd had very different life experiences from me. But there was no doubt about it: she could bake.

We'd been advertising the Winter Pastry Fest for a few weeks now, and customers seemed excited about the winter treats.

No one was more excited than Police Chief Westerman, who'd been a regular at the bakery since it opened. It helped that his office was right across the street at City Hall. If he could have a pneumatic tube installed to deliver beignets directly to his office, I'm sure he would. He'd already asked if he could put in a large order for a staff Christmas party at River Grove City Hall.

"It looks like we've got most of the ingredients," I said, as I thought about the items. "We've been promoting the heck out of this, so I know we're going to have more customers than usual. I don't want you to be overwhelmed. If anything goes wrong while I'm away, you'll text or call me, right?"

"But I know how hard you work, Gracie." She shook her head. "I don't want you to even think about The Laughing Loaf while you're gone."

I laughed. "Realistically, that's not going to happen, but thanks."

I went over to do stretch and folds in the dough in the sourdough tubs, trying to get on with my work. Then I noticed Beck was standing there, waiting. Like she wanted to ask me something else.

"What's up, Beck?"

"I was wondering if I could take another class." I was puzzled by her hesitation. I'd encouraged her to sign up for any classes she thought might help her.

"Of course you can, Beck. Did you find another pastry class?" I continued folding since it needed to get done now, for the timing of the bread cycle. Bread is a finicky taskmaster. "No problem. I'm sure we can work time into our schedule. I'll talk to Chloe."

She blinked at me coyly. "It's not a pastry class. There's this baker I've been following on YouTube. He's really cool. His specialty is sourdough bread. His name is Daniel

Bordleman. He explains how yeast works, kind of the science behind the bread. His videos are so funny—he dresses up as a mad scientist, or sometimes as Frankenstein. A book of his just came out—*Night of the Living Bread*."

I continued folding the dough in the tub. I was ten years older than Beck and suddenly felt old, out of touch with what people her age were tuning into on the internet. "Haven't heard of him."

Then I looked up at her suddenly. I realized what she'd been saying. "Wait a minute—did you say you want to take a bread class?"

"We have to juggle everything here just so you can go away." She looked sad. "I want to be able to fill in for you. And understand more about how to do the breads. I feel like it would make me a better employee."

Her thoughtfulness melted my heart. "Thank you, Beck. I appreciate that. Let's talk about this more. Where is this guy based?"

"He has a bakery up in Sonoma County. It's called Night Rose. They make amazing baked goods. Really cool flavors. They remind me of the flavors you do with your scones, Gracie, but I mean—they're really unusual combinations—like fennel and orange, black garlic and coriander. You should check out his YouTube channel. And his website." She pulled her phone out of her apron pocket and scrolled through some screens. I moved over to work with the brioche tubs.

As I watched her phone, the video began, fading in from a black screen. A light went on in a kitchen, lighting up a bearded man's face in eerie shadows. Music from a theremin played in the background, like a soundtrack from an old horror movie.

"Welcome to my bread lair," Daniel Bordleman said,

giving the camera a menacing look. The camera pulled back and a light went on, highlighting a big mixing bowl overflowing with gooey, bubbling dough.

"It...LIVES!" He cried out, lurching back from the bowl, his hand to his mouth. He faced the camera solemnly.

"I'm Daniel Bordleman, and this is... *Night of the Living Bread*. Coming to you from Night Rose bakery, in the spooky woods of Sonoma County in Northern California." Then he widened his eyes and added for emphasis, "At *night*."

I laughed and rolled my eyes at Beck. "Is this guy for real? He can't be serious."

Beck laughed. "He's a little over the top. He can be so funny. But I've learned a lot from his videos. He explains things in a way I can understand. So it's making more sense to me how you make the bread and why we feed the starter for the sourdough. I'm actually a lot more excited about breadmaking now."

Beck's brown eyes shone with excitement.

"It's so interesting, Gracie. Pastry—it's like creating art —and I love making beautiful, delicious pastries. But bread is a living thing. A creature! Daniel says when you have starter, you're really learning how to take care of a pet. To get the right flavors, you have to keep your dough at the right temperature. You feed it just the right amount at the right time. You make sure everything is perfect for it to be happy. It's all about time and temperature—and understanding what's going on in the dough."

This did sound intriguing. I wondered if Nate and I could make a visit to this guy's bakery on our trip to Sonoma.

"What about the classes?" I asked as I covered the tubs

and turned to slide them into the proofer. "Would you go up to the bakery to take them?"

Beck cast her eyes down. "The classes are all at the bakery, I checked. There aren't any until he's done with his book tour. So probably not till the spring."

"Maybe Nate and I will check out his bakery this weekend." Knowing Nate's love for bread, this would not be a hard sell. "If I meet him, I'll tell him you're a fan and interested in his classes. And, Beck, that's really kind of you to want to help with the bread."

Once our mid-morning slow period was over, I went out to help customers at the counter, some coming in out of the rain for a hot cup of coffee. Some had come in for fresh loaves of bread to take home for dinner.

Mayor Corinne Webster, at the counter, was reading messages on her phone. I greeted her cheerfully.

"Mayor C, good to see you. Hazelnut latte with oat milk, right? Kale Frittata?"

Our mayor didn't smile, just nodded curtly. She took many things very seriously: law and order in town, River Grove traditions, and lately, the River Grove softball team, called The River Grove River Rats. She was recruiting for the coming spring season and planned on starting team practices in the new year. I'd heard she'd been making her rounds, and I'd been avoiding her for that very reason.

"So Gracie, I'd like you to play on the team this year," she started in. "Last year, it sounded like you couldn't take the time off from the bakery."

"Running a business is a 24/7 thing," I said with a grim look on my face, resurrecting my excuse from last year. "I don't think I can get away for the practices—or the games on Saturdays." I shook my head. "Sorry. It sounds like a great group, Corinne."

Mayor C looked around the bakery and at Beck, who was singing to herself as she prepared the mayor's hazelnut latte at the espresso machine.

"It seems like you've got lots of help now. I saw Chloe Westerman and Aiden Franzi helping you out a few weeks ago. Things look like they're running very smoothly now."

As Mayor C looked at me expectantly, I rifled through my second-tier excuses, which were closer to the truth: I was not, in any way, an athlete. I did not know how to play softball, and I wasn't very interested in learning.

"You don't want me on your team," I said, frowning. "Didn't you say the team is usually near the top of the league? I'm really bad at it. I'll bring you guys down."

Mayor C shook her head. "Oh, Gracie. We can work on that." Her reply sounded ominous. It made me even less interested in playing. "What about Nate?"

I handed the mayor her latte and pulled a kale tarragon frittata cup out of the display case with tongs.

"What about him?"

"I heard he's quite an athlete. Would he be interested?"

I wasn't about to throw Nate under the bus so I could get out of playing on the team.

"Corinne, you'll have to ask him yourself."

The mayor gave me a disapproving look. She hadn't gotten the answer she wanted.

"Fine, Gracie. I guess I'll have to do that."

She picked up her latte and frittata and headed for a table. I sighed with relief.

Beck shot a look at me as she put the lids on two lattes. "Mayor C puts the pressure on everyone. Good for you for saying no."

. . .

Right after lunch, I saw a face I hadn't seen in a couple of months.

Kirk Schiffer, my friend Elana's husband. Under a heavy raincoat, he wore sweatpants and a hoodie with a logo for BlueSurf, the software company he ran in Santa Cruz. He must be working from home today. His lips were pressed tight. He shifted on his feet.

Before October, Elana and I had traded gossip on the goings on in River Grove, indulged our love for good wine and food, and tried our hand at solving mysterious goings on in our little town.

Elana had been my partner in crime.

But after the scary situation with the Russians at The Riverside Saloon in October, Elana thew up her hands and walked away from our friendship. Elana wasn't sure if I was some kind of criminal—or if I was maybe fleeing an abusive relationship. She was upset that I couldn't talk about it. What kind of a person keeps secrets like this from their best friend? I totally understood Elana's frustration. Along with my father, I was in federal witness protection, and I had to keep my past secret.

I sucked it up and tried hard to smile at Kirk.

"Kirk. Good to see you. What can I get you?"

"Hi, Gracie." He cleared his throat. "Got any brioche? Elana's sister is coming into town. We're going to make brunch Saturday morning. I can't make French toast without your brioche."

I looked toward the espresso machine where Beck stood. She'd heard the conversation, though she tried to keep her head down, working a little too diligently at cleaning the milk spout.

"I've got one loaf left from today," I cautioned him, keeping my voice quiet. "This is the last bread we have for a while since I'll be out of town through the weekend. Beck's doing only pastries while I'm gone."

He looked at me gratefully. "Thanks, Gracie. I—uh, we really appreciate it."

I don't know why I said it. The words just came out of me.

"I miss her."

Kirk shoved his hands in the pockets of his sweatpants nervously and shook his head. He seemed to have trouble meeting my eyes.

"Uh, yeah. You two need to talk."

A little shaken by Kirk's comment, I took a moment to brood over my coffee, then threw myself into my duties.

I peeked in on the loaves in the proofer. Then I slid another tray of cinnamon rolls into the oven. We always sold more cinnamon rolls when the weather was chilly and wet, so I'd gotten used to preparing for this. There was nothing as comforting on a rainy day as eating a fresh-from-the oven cinnamon roll.

I rotated the sourdough tub, giving it another fold, then turned the tub. I inhaled the rich, fermented smell, which in some way, reminds me of the smell of a deep, rich red wine.

I looked at the calendar pinned up on the wall of the back room. Beck had drawn smiley faces and snowflakes on the days I'd be gone and had scrawled across them GRACIE'S GETAWAY!

Nate and I had been through a lot since we'd met, which had been right after his brother Nico had been killed behind my bakery. This weekend's trip together was a big step forward for us.

It had been two-and-a-half years since I'd turned in my ex-husband Ben for selling tech defense secrets back in Seattle. One night, I'd found a list of bank deposits on his computer, sent from various foreign governments: Russia, China, North Korea.

After I testified against Ben in court, Federal marshals helped my father and me relocate to the small town of River Grove, in the Northern California redwoods, with new identities. I went from being Grace Kristen Morrison, to Gracie Katherine Markley.

My father, my little dog and I had been in witness protection for almost two years, with all the weirdness and secrecy that came with that. Time and counseling had helped me deal with my marriage's sudden crash and burn, but I couldn't say I was over it.

How had I made such a mistake in my choice of a partner? I'd been married to Ben for eight years—since right after college. I hadn't known he was capable of such greed and deception. He'd even threatened to say I was his accomplice if I tried to turn him in.

With all that, I was a little wary about getting involved with someone else, even someone who seemed as kind and down-to-earth as Nate.

I wished I could talk to my friend Elana about this.

As WE EXPERIENCED a lull in customers, I went back to slide our last tray of cinnamon rolls into the oven.

Beck came into the back room and went to her wicker basket on the stool next to the industrial fridge. She pulled out a large hardbacked book.

"Gracie, since you might be seeing Daniel and his bakery, I'd like you to take this. It's his new baking book, *Night of the Living Bread*."

I took the book from her and began leafing through the pages.

The cover featured a heavily shadowed black and white photo of Daniel, with a pointy goatee, round brown eyes and heavy unibrow, staring into a bowl of dough, looking a lot like the intro to the YouTube video Beck had shown me on her phone. There were chapters explaining in simple terms how bread worked—from what yeast was, to how it interacted with bacteria in the mix to affect flavor and rise. Then some interesting recipes for basic dough and what looked like a variety of bread methods. There was one of my favorites, biga (which I'd named my dog after), poolish, ciabatta, and sourdough and starter-based breads. I was interested in finding out more about his methods—and wanted to compare his sourdough to The Laughing Loaf's. I hoped I'd get to meet Daniel when we went up to Sonoma.

I set the timer in my pocket for the cinnamon rolls. "Beck, you've obviously been bitten by the bread bug. I'll take a look at Daniel's book. Of course, you can take a class from him. Let's work that into our schedule for when Daniel's done with his book tour. We can see if Chloe and Aiden can come back and fill in."

I knew I'd eventually have to hire someone—someone who didn't have high school classes, so they could work at the bakery during the day. I hoped I could find someone who could work well with Beck and I. It would definitely help if they liked to bake while singing along to 80s pop music.

Everything was on track for me and Nate to go away over the weekend. I was thankful that Chloe and Aiden could work tomorrow. It was staff development day at the high school—no classes. Beck would get some valuable experience managing employees.

Everything was falling into place.

Beck finally feeling confident about managing the bakery? Check.

Weekend help from Chloe and Aiden? Check.

Extra sugar and chocolate ordered? Check.

Nate had asked me a few months back about going away together, but he'd given me lots of space about it. Lots of time to think, to get Beck and the bakery ready, and to mentally prepare.

Which was perfect because I really needed it.

I WAS LEAVING town for a three-day weekend. This was our busiest time of year. I felt, as my British dad liked to say— that I was *bunking off*. Going off with my boyfriend while Beck, with Chloe and Aiden's help, worked hard to keep things running.

Beck smiled over the metal table at me as she assembled apple tarts for refrigerating till tomorrow morning's bake. "How are you feeling about this weekend? Getting excited?"

I looked down at the brioche dough, feeling its silky smoothness as I shaped it into loaves. My emotions right now were complicated. Tears lurked in the corners of my eyes, ready to come out at the slightest trigger.

"I've never taken a break from this place. It'll feel strange to not be here."

Beck arranged apple slices over the tart shells. "My mom used to tell me when we were homeschooling and when I was working on a project—take a break. Go for a walk in the woods. Do something different. Give your mind a sabbath. That's what she called it. When you come back, your mind will be rested. You'll see things differently."

Beck and I had very different upbringings. I grew up in

an urban environment, the only child of an overeducated professor and a music teacher; I'd traveled all over the world. Beck had been homeschooled with her many brothers and had never left the tiny town of River Grove. I got a little tired of hearing nuggets of her mother's advice, but Beck was loyal, hardworking and wise in ways I wasn't. Sometimes I unfairly discounted her experience.

In this case, she was right. My trip would give me a needed break from my bakery business.

It was what would happen after I got back that would make for a lot of work.

Chapter Two

Thursday evening, December 5

On Thursday afternoon of that week, I stayed late at the bakery, while Beck prepped scones and tarts and mixed the beignet dough. I made a large batch of cranberry orange scones, since that was something I could do with my eyes closed—and they were on Beck's menu. I cut them into triangles on trays and stacked them in the freezer so Beck would have an easy bake-up during my time away if she needed it.

I heard teenagers passing by on the sidewalk on their way back from RG's Pizza down the street. Laughter and shouting. With Beck hard at work on her creations, the bakery felt too quiet. I went into the gated area off of the back room, where I cuddled with Biga for a few minutes. I'd been busy all day, so he was giving me hurt looks for a while, until I pulled out the treats. Then he was all over me.

I wished I could invite Elana to come over and share a bottle of wine in the dining room, so I could process my thoughts about my getaway with Nate.

By 4:30 p.m., Beck and I had prepped all we could for

the next day. I wiped down tables and counters and mopped the dining area floor. Beck's husband Sam, drenched from the rain, stood outside the back door to pick her up. He wiped his work boots on the doormat and shook himself off so he wouldn't drip on the floor.

"Come on in, Sam," I called as I loaded pans and utensils into the dishwasher.

"Hey, Gracie." Sam waved as he stepped inside. Beck was wrapping a tub of cinnamon roll dough for its overnight chill in the fridge. "Nate's been talking about your trip." Nate lived on the same street as Beck and Sam. Since Nate had moved to River Grove, the two had become friends. They'd worked together to convert the shed on Nate's property into a photo studio. "He's pretty excited. He was nervous about choosing the right place to stay in Sonoma."

"Really?" I gave him a curious look.

"Nate would sleep in a sleeping bag in a tent if he could," Sam laughed. "He knows that's not your thing. He wants to make sure it's special for you. The guy kept showing me places, asking me if I thought you'd like them."

After eight years with someone like Ben, I had leveled up.

Between this and leaving my bakery for the first time, those lurking tears were ready to flow.

I willed myself to smile.

"Thanks for telling me that, Sam."

AFTER PACKAGING up some of Beck's pumpkin beignets, Sam and Beck were headed over to her parents' house for a birthday dinner for one of her many older brothers. Was it four brothers? Five? I knew it was a lot. I'd lost count.

My phone vibrated with a text.

I pulled it out of my pocket to see Nate's words. He photographed birds for a living, and it took him all over the world. In October, he'd gone to the Galapagos Islands to photograph finches for a coffee table book. Today, he'd gone to the coast to get shots of egrets for a nature conservancy advertising campaign.

> On my way back from the shoot at Montara. Soaked and freezing. Checking in —ready for Sonoma?

I SMILED and felt that weird fluttering in my chest. Anticipation. Joy. And maybe terror.

> I'm set. Bakery's covered for the trip! Come over for dinner?

> Brandy with your dad will warm me up.

> Warning - He's on dinner duty. See you at 6!

* * *

MY FATHER, as part of his new life as a man who made his own food, was in the kitchen. He bustled around in an apron, consulting a handwritten recipe stained with sauce. He set about preheating and measuring everything precisely—holding filled measuring cups up to his eyes to make sure the contents were precisely level.

"What are you making? You've been very mysterious

about it." I pulled out a wooden cutting board and began slicing a loaf of Laughing Loaf sourdough. The kitchen smelled like cheesy goodness and aromatic Italian herbs.

He turned to me, his glasses fogged by steam from the boiling pot of pasta.

"Chicken Tetrazzini. Mary Jo's recipe. Oh, and I've got a salad in the refrigerator." Mary Jo Hartman, a widow and the proprietor of River Grove's Growing Affection nursery, had been spending time with my father over the past year.

"Sounds like a great dinner, dad." I pulled a bottle of brandy down from the liquor cabinet, along with a dry Viognier, a white wine, for dinner. "Nate says he's bringing dessert."

My Brit father leveled a serious look at me. "You're really doing this. Leaving."

"Well, yeah." I gave him an amused look. My father was absentminded but not that absentminded. "Tomorrow morning."

"Don't think I don't know. You two are bunking off to go snog somewhere."

I turned beet red, indignant. "Bunking off? I've worked at the bakery every day for almost two years. I never slack off. It's two and a half days."

My dad laughed and turned to me, spaghetti claw in hand, his eyes unreadable behind his fogged-up glasses. A corner of his mouth turned up mischievously.

"It's about time, my dear."

"Whatever, Dad." I rolled my eyes, feeling about Chloe Westerman's age. "I'm looking forward to this. I need a break. Especially after everything that happened to us in October."

"I'm happy for you both." His smile was genuine. "Mary Jo might come over while you're gone, by the way."

He watched my face. Was he trying to read my reaction? It wasn't like I disliked Mary Jo that much; it was that I compared her with my mother, who'd passed away when I was fifteen.

Mary Jo was the first serious relationship my father had had since then. She was loud, read a lot of celebrity gossip and smelled like cigarette smoke—very different than my mother. Still, she made him happy, though from what he'd told me, she'd broken up with him at least twice in the past year and a half. I guess things were back on.

"I hope you guys have a lovely time," I said as graciously as I could, as I arranged the sliced sourdough in a wicker basket and put it on the table. "And make sure you stay out of trouble."

My father chuckled as he scooped up a tangle of spaghetti to test it for doneness. He set the colander up in the sink and took the pot over to drain the pasta.

"You won't be here to find out if we do." He was pushing back at me--which I deserved. I needed to let go and let him make his own decisions. Part of my fear was that I didn't want my head-in-the-clouds professor father to let something slip about our witness protection status. A few drinks, a little snogging and he might spill the beans to Mary Jo about our situation.

I looked up at the kitchen clock. Ever-punctual Nate would be here in about twenty minutes. I peeled the foil off the bottle of Viognier then stabbed the corkscrew into the cork and started turning. It was a bottle Elana had given me, a gift from a trip she and Kirk had made to Napa earlier this year.

Nate, because he was Nate, biked over in the rain and showed up on our front porch in a poncho, dripping wet. He left his bike leaning against the front of the house, sheltered by the eaves. He pulled a plastic bag with an intriguing citrus smell out of his backpack.

"I'll take that for you." I smiled and immediately peered into the bag and took a deep breath.

"Lemon tarts from a shop in Half Moon Bay."

"Excellent choice, Nate. You've hit my dad's sweet spot —and mine."

Nate refused to come inside until he'd stripped down to his dry clothes. I looked appreciatively at his arms, muscles visible under his sweater.

"Something smells amazing in here," Nate announced as he stepped into our entry way, kissing up just a little to my dad. My dad had just slid the tetrazzini, pasta and chicken covered in cheese and cream sauce, into the oven. Just inside the doorway, Nate hugged me and lingered for a moment, kissing me on the forehead. I sunk my face into his wool sweater. He smelled like pine trees and sea air. "Stay right there, Gracie—you're keeping me warm," Nate whispered in my ear.

"It's chicken tetrazzini, Nate. After doing some research, I optimized the recipe," my dad called out from the kitchen proudly, as if he'd just made a major scientific discovery. "I've added some panko crumbs to the top for a better mouthfeel."

I snorted at this and even Nate looked down at the ground, trying to keep a straight face. I wondered what Mary Jo would think of him "optimizing" her recipe. My father, who sounded like he was ready for his own Food Network show, wiped his hands on a dish towel. "Nate, you look like you could use some brandy."

"Is it that obvious?" Nate grinned.

My father handed a snifter of brandy to Nate, who

settled in next to me on the sofa. Biga, who'd been waiting for his chance, jumped up on his lap.

"I'm finally thawing out. Thank you." Nate stroked Biga's back. "It was worth the freezing rain. The clouds helped me get some dramatic shots. I wished you could have seen the snowy egrets."

I smiled at him slyly. "The bakery was so nice and warm today." He gave me a mock punch in the arm.

"I just sent you a photo of the place where we're staying in Sonoma." He set his brandy down on the end table and pulled out his phone. "On the Bodega Highway. It's a very fancy hut. I'd be fine with just a hut, but I thought you'd probably appreciate the fancy part." He scrolled through photos on the rental site. He landed on an adorable small, white house, with a fenced front porch and a porch swing. The place was surrounded by trees and set far back on the road on some land. One photo taken at night, showed the back deck lined with strings of lights.

"This is beautiful. And I wouldn't really say that's a hut," I said gratefully. I was not a huge fan of roughing it. Then I remembered my conversation with Beck today. "There's a bakery up there—called Night Rose. Would you be up for checking it out? Daniel, the owner, has videos on YouTube, and Beck is obsessed with him. He sounds like a really interesting person. His bread's supposed to be amazing."

Nate laughed, that rich, deep laugh I loved. "You think I'm going to turn down bread?"

My father hadn't just been bragging. Dinner was delicious. I admitted it: Mary Jo must be a decent cook to have crafted the recipe. Nate had seconds, and I mopped up the remaining sauce from my plate with a slice of sourdough.

After dinner, Nate and I cleared the table and loaded

the dishwasher. After we finished off our lemon tarts, Nate challenged my dad to a game of chess.

"John, you know you want to play," Nate said with challenge in his voice. Barely containing his excitement, my dad hurried to his study to get his chess case.

After he'd set up the board with white and black marble pieces, he looked across at Nate, crossed his arms and gave him a bold stare, looking like a villain in a Bond film.

"Nate, I'm afraid I'm going to have to take you down."

I lay on the couch watching them with sleepy amusement as I finished my wine. With my early hours at the bakery, I'd been awake almost sixteen hours. My dad was in a feisty mood tonight, trash talking as Nate went after his king.

"You think that move's going to protect you?" He chuckled. "Think again, son."

A few moves later, I heard my dad.

"And—that is *checkmate*."

As I knew all too well, my dad was tough to beat.

After my dad settled into his chair to read, I walked Nate outside to the porch. It was dark and chilly, but the rain had stopped. I could hear the San Luciano River behind us, gushing over the rocks, loud and full from last week's rains. The air smelled like wet trees. If a scent had a color, it smelled like a deep, rich green.

After we engaged in some prolonged snogging on the front porch out of my dad's sight, Nate held me close.

"Gracie." He smiled, his voice low. "I know you made a lot of arrangements so we could get away. I don't take that for granted."

After he took off on his bike, I stood on the porch for a few minutes, inhaling the fresh, damp air. My insides rippled with excitement—and the fear of some of the things we'd talk about on our trip.

I wanted Nate to know me. Who I really was and what I'd lived through.

I stayed out on the porch for a while in the cool stillness after the cleansing rain. Over the past two years, so much had been washed away. My ex-husband Ben and his selfishness, my old attitudes about who I was as a wife and even as a daughter.

The things I'd been through in the past two years had changed me. Life was better because of it.

I took a deep, rich breath of cool air.

Chapter Three

Biga knew something was up.

That night, he ignored my dad, snubbing him when he wanted to cuddle with him in the easy chair. My dog stuck by my side, pressing his little body up against me on the bed as I packed my suitcase. Every time I left the room to get toiletries or something from the dryer, he followed me.

"Biga, I love you, too. But I need to get things ready." I picked him up and carried him in the laundry basket on my way back to my room. He rode in the basket, holding his head up as he surveyed the room, like an emperor in his sedan chair.

"It's two and a half days." I scratched his back affectionately after he jumped out onto the bed. "I promise I'm coming back."

Biga gave me a skeptical look. *You say that. But how can I know for sure? Sometimes Papa reads his books and forgets about me.*

Now to pack.

I pulled clothing options out of my closet. I picked out a

green and brown plaid jacket that brought out my hazel eyes. I held it up and looked in the mirror. I threw it on the pile to take. Then a tan skirt that showed a nice amount of leg. And a couple pairs of jeans, since I knew we'd end up on a hike to find birds.

I packed hiking boots I'd worn when Ben and I did an eight-day hike up Kilimanjaro, and a pair of fancy leather boots for going out to dinner.

I wished I had Elana giving me advice on what to wear.

I lay down on the bed and found the address of the Night Rose bakery in Daniel Bordleman's book and plugged it into my phone. Like our rental house, Night Rose was on the Bodega Highway, which ran between Sebastopol and Highway 1, which connected to the coast.

I read about the bakery, which didn't have a set menu; you showed up and chose from what the staff baked—a lot of it was determined by what Daniel felt like baking that day. That might be anything from apricot pistachio biga and black garlic loaves to banana praline scones. Everything was baked in a woodfired oven.

He must be doing something right. I checked Night Rose out on Yelp. The bakery had a cumulative rating of 4.9 stars.

Daniel's introduction to the book described how he'd become a baker. Like me, he had no formal culinary education. He'd worked at several small bakeries, then launched out on his own after a falling out with his baking partner over "decision-making issues." There was a lot of swagger in Daniel's words. He stated that in any disagreements with co-workers and partners, he was always right. The man didn't lack confidence, that was for sure.

I slipped *Night of the Living Bread* book into my messenger bag. I was intrigued by the guy. It would be interesting to meet him and see how another bakery was run, especially one that had earned high praise from restaurant critics. Maybe I could learn from him.

My phone lit up with a text.

See you at 9 a.m. Sleep well, G

You, too.

I set my suitcase and messenger bag by my door and prepared for bed.

I went out to say goodnight to my dad, who sat in his easy chair, reading a book on quantum mechanics. Just a little light reading before bedtime.

When he saw me, he shut the book and took off his glasses, which was unusual for him. He looked up at me.

"You're all ready, dear?"

"Packed and ready to go. I'm nervous." I told him that I was going to ask Nate about our ride back from the airport and try to figure out why he had called me by my old name —and how much he knew about my past. My father was the only person on the face of the earth I could talk to about this, aside from the federal marshals assigned to us, Maura and Jeremy.

"Wouldn't it be easier not to know?" My father furrowed his brow, genuinely puzzled. "Nate already cares about you. He's a good man. Does it matter?"

"I want to know how much he knows," I said. "Maybe he isn't the local federal marshals' contact, keeping an eye on us. He couldn't be, if he was in the Galapagos when the Russians showed up here. But maybe he has some other connection."

My father sighed and gave me a look over his glasses. I

know he wished I didn't have to find out everything. He had his own need to know, but in his case, it was limited to functions, equations, and the laws of physics—not human relationships.

"Can you do me a favor, dear?" He looked up at me from his seat. "Relax and try to have a good time."

I smiled and kissed his forehead.

"And dad, be careful while I'm gone. Keep the doors locked. Please don't open the door unless you know who it is. Watch out for Biga. We'll be back Sunday afternoon." I secretly hoped Mary Jo Hartman wasn't here when I got back.

"You're not going into the bakery as soon as you get back, are you?"

I laughed and rubbed my sleepy eyes. "Beck's in charge. It's Winter Pastry Fest. I might as well enjoy my time off and do nothing."

My dad gave me an amused look. "Are you capable of doing nothing, dear?"

Point taken, dad.

I went back to my room and turned out the light.

Biga wedged himself in next to me with a little snort.

Then we were both down for the count.

* * *

Friday, *December 6*

I woke up at 4 a.m., before cyemembering it wasn't a typical workday and Nate wasn't picking me up till 9 a.m.

My body was synchronized to baker's hours, and it was going to be hard to convince it: *No really, it's okay; you can sleep in.*

After tossing back and forth and trying to get comfortable, I picked up *Night of the Living Bread* and read through Daniel Bordleman's chapter on his baking philosophy, which like his bread, seemed full of hot air (pun intended). He talked about how important good technique was to making superior bread. He threw some shade at a former bakery partner. I did appreciate the simple way he explained the bread process, the science behind it, and how time and temperature work their magic on bread to create great flavor. I could see why Beck would want to learn from him.

The book had some interesting recipes that I wanted to try. Like me, Daniel experimented with unusual ingredients and flavors. He had a pumpkin bread made with seeds and ancient grains that had a great texture, judging by the photos. I wanted to try some when we visited Night Rose, though, with the way Daniel ran the bakery, who knew if they'd be featuring that bread when we visited.

Since Beck had found out about the classes from Daniel's YouTube channel, I watched some of his videos.

At 6:30 a.m., I finally got to sleep. I slept for a little over an hour and woke feeling rested.

NATE PICKED ME UP, typical of him, at 9 on the dot. He'd made me a cappuccino at home that tasted as good as anything Beck or I had made at The Laughing Loaf. It was even neatly packaged in an eco-friendly, reusable cup and lid.

I hugged my dad, cuddled Biga for a few minutes, then Nate and I were on our way.

As sun filtered through the redwoods around us, we followed Highway 9 over to Highway 1, then drove up the coast. The fog was burning off, revealing openings of clear blue sky. The air felt fresh and clean, cool but not cold. After yesterday's fears about leaving the bakery, my heart felt light. I leaned back in my seat, watching the scenery. And out of the corner of my eye, I watched Nate's muscular arms as he steered his hybrid SUV through the curves on the coastal highway.

"Must feel strange," Nate said, as we came in sight of the coast near Pacifica. "Not being at The Laughing Loaf this morning."

"It's like playing hooky. It was hard to feel okay about it at first—now I'm fully on board."

Nate glanced over at me, a playful look on his face. "I'll support you. I won't take any photos on the trip."

"Really?" I gave him a sly look. "We are going over the Golden Gate Bridge in the next hour. You're not going to get a shot of that view?"

"Watch me." Nate looked straight ahead, but his lips twisted into a smile.

"If you see an intriguing heron, you are so pulling off the road, Nathaniel Behrens. You won't be able to stop yourself."

Nate was a bird nerd. Birds fascinated him, and his photos of them in flight and in their natural habitats were breathtaking.

"Excuse me, but I think I can resist that." Nate raised an eyebrow. "This is a getaway for us. I can photograph birds any time."

"Now I feel a little guilty checking out Daniel's bakery." I watched as the coast flashing past us switched to rocky cliffs. "That's research for my job."

"If I didn't like bread so much, I'd agree with you. But now that you showed me that cookbook, I want to try everything this guy makes."

. . .

AFTER WE CROSSED the Golden Gate Bridge, Nate pulled into the observation parking on the Marin side.

It was a gorgeous day, with the rust-colored bridge looking majestic against a blue sky with billowing, whipped cream clouds. The place was stunning, from the skyline of San Francisco on one end to the rich green Marin Headlands on the north end. Even the restrooms. The window in the women's restroom on this side of the bridge had one of the best scenic views I'd ever seen.

We took selfies with the gorgeous bridge behind us. He used his camera; I used my phone. We made silly faces and pretended to grab at the bridge looming over us. I took a selfie of him on his knees, with me standing over him, like I was the giant. I almost got hit by an old man wobbling off the bridge on his bike—Nate captured the scene with his camera. We scrolled through our photos and laughed so hard we almost cried.

Night Rose was on the way to our rental, so around 12:30 p.m. Nate wheeled into the bakery's gravel parking lot and snagged the last open spot.

The bakery was in a converted red barn, with a faded image of its name circling a red rose in bloom. It looked like an old produce sign from the 1940s.

Next to the barn was a grassy area with picnic tables. Every table was filled with customers enjoying sandwiches and baked treats from Night Rose. There was a line of customers at a folksy-looking screen door, which looked like it was supposed to be the main entrance. Tantalizing smells of fresh baked bread drifted out into the cool air.

"Nate, we can come back after we've checked into the

hut." I wasn't sure how long we'd be waiting for lunch. "This could take a while."

"I'm fine with waiting. It's not like we've got anything specific planned."

We took our places in the line. The woman in front of us turned to us. "If you guys haven't been here before, you've got to try the pastrami sandwich with the dill havarti bread. It's one of the things they serve regularly for lunch. It's amazing."

Nate and I looked at each other and shrugged.

"Sounds great," I responded with a smile.

"I'm down with that," Nate said, peering wistfully through the door to the bakery offerings visible beyond us. "As long as we can pick out a few other things to take with us. I mean, we'll need to have breakfast for two days, and lunch—"

The line finally moved us through the door. I'd been looking forward to seeing what the place looked like inside. As soon as we came in, we saw a very long counter, with one of the biggest display cases I'd seen. Hung above the counter was a huge chalkboard menu, embellished by hand-drawn blue crescent moons, gold stars and red roses. In the cavernous space beyond the counter, employees shaped loaves on metal tables and mixed dough in tubs.

I saw at least three large brick woodfired ovens set into the far wall. A glove-clad baker slid in a long-handled metal peel and pulled out a dark brown batard of bread.

Nate scanned the board and gulped. "I have decision paralysis. Everything I see looks good."

I turned to him. "That just means we'll have to come back tomorrow."

He pulled me close and kissed the top of my head. "That attitude is one of the many reasons I like you."

We ordered two of the dill havarti pastrami sandwiches, a couple of interestingly flavored scones, a loaf of ancient grains pumpkin bread and a country sourdough loaf. I wanted Beck and I to do a taste test to compare Night Rose's sourdough with The Laughing Loaf's.

I was paying for the order at the register, when I spotted a man with a dark goatee who looked just like the face on the dramatic cover of *Night of the Living Bread*. He tapped the shoulder of the young, red-haired woman at the register.

I could hear his voice, hissing in her ear.

"If you do that again, Maeve—so help me—you're *out*. How many times have we talked about this?" The look on his face was menacing, like something out of one of his horror-based baking videos.

"You must be Daniel." I called out as cheerfully as I could, partly in an attempt to rescue the poor woman, whose eyes were wide with terror.

The baker turned to me, and the dark look on his face faded, quickly replaced by a cordial smile.

"Yes, I'm Daniel Bordleman. Owner of Night Rose."

"My name is Gracie Markley, and this is Nate Behrens. I run The Laughing Loaf bakery, down in River Grove in the Santa Cruz Mountains. My assistant manager Beck is a big fan of your YouTube videos. She's been raving about them."

Daniel broke into a smile that looked condescending. "Ah, Gracie. A fellow baker. Just starting out?" His tone and tilted head rubbed me the wrong way. So maybe I was a little forceful in my response.

"Actually, I've been running my bakery for almost two years, Daniel. We started making a profit six months ago. Like you, I'm self-taught."

Daniel looked startled by my reply. He chuckled to himself. "Good for you, Gracie."

After we finished our transaction, he went to the end of the counter and opened a low gate for us to enter. "Please let me show you around our bakery. Then, why don't you bring your sandwiches upstairs and join me for lunch in my studio?"

We walked through a low gate into the huge baking room where everything was happening. The smells were off the hook. From the smoky scent of the woodfired ovens to the yeasty smell of fresh bread. Fragrances of garlic, fresh herbs, lavender, orange and lemon from assistants zesting and dicing at long tables.

"Night Rose is open seven days a week. Customers come to us from all over California. All over the country, actually. They come here because we are unique. All ingredients are locally sourced, and all of it's organic. We grow our herbs on site. We started the classes last year mostly because there was such a demand to learn my techniques."

"I've been reading *Night of the Living Bread*," I said, as Daniel cast a critical eye over an assistant who was chopping chives. The young assistant looked up at Daniel with fear in his eyes and immediately adjusted the position of his knife. "I'm excited to try some of the recipes."

Daniel put out his hand expectantly, a look of contempt on his face, and the young assistant reluctantly gave him the knife. "Rafal, after all our training, I can't believe you're still not doing it right." He turned to me, and in a flash, a pleasant smile appeared on his face. "I'm giving a demonstration tomorrow morning on woodfired baking. You're welcome to join us."

After the conversation Nate and I had in the car about both of us leaving work behind, I was ready to say no. But

Nate gave me a look and nodded. "If you want to, do it, Gracie."

I turned to Daniel.

"Nate and I came up here to get away. But I'll think about it, thanks."

"Starts in here tomorrow morning at 7:30 a.m.," Daniel explained. "Which is probably much later than the baker's hours you normally keep. We finish the class before we open at 8:30. It won't take long."

The thought of baking in a woodfired oven filled me with excitement. I wanted to spend time with Nate, definitely, but this was an opportunity to learn from a master in my field. The thought of learning something new from him excited me.

Nate must have realized that. He leaned into me, and I breathed in the fresh scent of his skin.

"You get the woodfired ovens, I get a hike at Bodega Bay with my camera bright and early. Deal?"

I slipped my hand into his.

"Deal."

After we watched the woodfired ovens in action, Daniel led us upstairs to a large studio, with a green screen, a high-tech digital recording setup and lots of props that looked like they'd been stolen from the set of a 1950s horror movie.

He flipped the light switch, and the room was flooded with light. A desk and files sat at one end of the studio, and several comfortable office chairs were set up around the desk.

"Have a seat, friends," Daniel gestured toward the chairs. "I'm going downstairs to grab my sandwich, and I'll be right back up."

We ate our sandwiches and drank bottled water, while waiting for Daniel.

"Damn, this is good bread." Nate closed his eyes and savored his sandwich. "The creamy havarti with the fresh dill. Just enough pastrami so it's not overwhelming."

I took a gulp of cold water from the bottle. "Did Daniel's treatment of his employees seem strange to you?"

"What was he saying to the woman at our register?" Nate asked after swallowing the last bite of his sandwich.

"He was threatening her."

"You're a better boss than Daniel." Nate smiled, a playful look in his light blue eyes, as he reached over to squeeze my hand.

"Oh, God. I would hope so." I frowned. "Because that's a pretty low bar."

IN FIVE MINUTES, Daniel Bordleman bounded back into his studio office, wrapped sandwich in hand.

He sat down at his desk and smiled at us both. I have no idea why he was giving us special attention. Maybe my cheeky response to him about my experience had earned his respect. For whatever reason, he'd decided he liked us. He peeled off the white paper and flattened it out under his sandwich.

"What do you think of the place?" Daniel asked, looking back and forth between Nate and I.

I quickly swallowed my bite of sandwich. "Your offerings are so varied here, and I love your flavor choices. I can't imagine running an operation as big as this."

"I worked my way up, Gracie. Started with small bakeries, but I knew what I wanted someday, and I never let anyone stand in my way. I've achieved what I wanted here at Night Rose. No thanks to my staff." He raised his eyebrows. "And now with the book—"

"My assistant Beck has been studying your book to learn about bread," I said with a smile. "She wants to take a sourdough class from you."

He peeled a pickle slice off his sandwich and tossed it on the paper wrap. He shook his head. "There's no way I can do classes while I'm on my book tour. I'm booked well into next year."

"Where are you going on your book tour?"

Daniel sat back and sighed. "December is the Bay Area and Monterey, then down the Central Coast to Santa Barbara and Pasadena."

"Any chance you're coming to Santa Cruz?"

"I'm doing a signing at a bookstore there next weekend."

"I know it's a last-minute request, Daniel. We're just a few miles from Santa Cruz. Would you consider teaching a sourdough class at The Laughing Loaf?" I leaned forward in my seat, waiting for what would probably be a big fat NO. Nate looked on with amusement. "You could film a video for your YouTube channel at our bakery. Our little mountain town in the redwoods is gorgeous. It's an old logging town. You could do a recipe from your new book for the class and get some promotion in before your talk at the bookstore."

Daniel Bordleman leaned back in his seat, his hand on his chin, his dark eyebrows furrowed, a faint smile on his face. "Interesting idea. A crazy idea. Let's talk about this after the demonstration tomorrow."

After finishing our sandwiches, Nate and I took our bags of baked goods and headed for the car, to start our actual getaway together. Excitement rippled through me. I'd just snagged the opportunity to have a world-famous baker teach a class at The Laughing Loaf.

Now I'd get to spend the next two days with a man I was crazy about.

Nate and I drove down Bodega Highway to our rental "hut." I rolled down the car window to smell the air, fresh and cool, as we drove through the tree-filled landscape.

As my hair did in damp weather, it cramped up into curls. Curls that always seemed to have a mind of their own. I smoothed it all down and pulled it back into a hair tie.

Nate glanced over at me, a look of curiosity on his face. "Why did you do that? Your hair looked great."

I shrugged. "I can't control it. It does its own thing."

A deep laugh rolled out of Nate as he gave me an admiring look.

"Then let it."

OUR HUT—A very small white farmhouse set back from the road—was adorable. Just a living room, a well-equipped kitchen, a bathroom, and a bedroom. It felt like we were playing house. The thought reverberated through my mind as I walked through it:

What if this was our house?

We investigated the fenced-in wooden deck out back, which had two comfortable chaise lounges lined up side by side, and a small table. In one corner of the deck, a wide stone bench circled a big propane-fueled fire pit.

There was a bucket filled with ice on the table, and in it a bottle of champagne.

"Should we save it for later?" But I already had my hands around it, reading the label and realizing this was a really good bottle of champagne.

Nate came up behind me and kissed the back of my neck.

"We're miles away from your dad's watchful eye, Gracie. And your dog's. We are alone. Nobody from River Grove to see us holding hands and start gossiping about it. Isn't that worth celebrating? Let's open it now."

I handed him the bottle and the towel and he loosened the cork, which popped out with a satisfying *thwop*.

I poured each of us a glass. We clinked our glasses together and sat down, side by side, on a single chaise, because each of us sitting in our own felt too far away. We leaned into each other, feeling each other's warmth as we drank.

I looked into his light blue eyes. When was it right to ask him what he knew about my past?

After finishing our glasses, Nate turned to me and pressed his lips against mine. I felt the soft scratch of his beard against my cheek. I felt completely content.

Soon I forgot I wanted to ask him anything.

* * *

WE BOTH TOOK A LONG NAP, something I wasn't in the habit of doing. Unfortunately, a baker's life doesn't allow for midday naps. It felt decadent and luxurious.

Then we drove east, into Sebastopol, to get groceries and a good bottle of local red wine for dinner. Nate had decided to use the propane grill, which was outside in a bricked-in area with a prep counter, next to the deck. He marinated tri-tip, and had it cooked and resting after the sun dipped down below the horizon. I prepared a salad and roasted potatoes inside in the oven.

I found the switch to turn on the deck lights and the entire back of the house lit up, looking festive—funny for this place that felt out in the middle of nowhere.

As soon as we sat down, I realized how cold it had gotten after the sun went down. The wind soon kicked up, rustling through the trees around us, and adding to the chill.

"I'll get some blankets." I set my wine glass down and ran inside and found a fluffy comforter in the armoire the owners had left for cold nights. We draped ourselves in it and huddled around the fire pit to eat our dinner. The woods around us smelled of eucalyptus and damp earth. Crickets sang to us. A peace settled over me that I hadn't felt in months.

"I had no idea it would be this cold," Nate said as we started eating. In the gold glow from the fire pit flame, I saw concern on his face. "You're shivering."

I shook my head. "The wine is helping and so's the fire. If it gets colder, I'll give up and go inside. But I like it out here."

Nate took a big sip from his wine glass and stretched out his long legs.

"When I was a kid, my family went on camping trips. Nico, me, and our parents. The funny thing was, there was always one thing that went wrong." Nate smiled to himself. "But that's the part we told stories about for years. The time we left our lighter and firewood at home. The time it suddenly rained in the middle of the night and capsized our tent."

I pictured young Nate valiantly trying to save the day, rubbing sticks together to make sparks to start a fire. Scrambling to secure a temporary tarp shelter over the tent and salvage the trip. Nate would do those things. He would know *how* to do those things.

"What about you? Did your family go camping when you were growing up?" Nate set his glass down on the deck and reached for my hand under the quilt. When his hand closed around mine, a shiver of excitement ran through me.

"Are you kidding? You know my dad. Would he sleep in a tent?" I laughed and Nate joined in. "My mom was an indoors girl. She loved her kitchen and her baby grand. The only way I learned to camp was in Girl Scouts. I went to summer camp on an island in the sound."

Nate shot me a curious look, frowned, then stared into the fire. I realized that while I had one parent left, Nate had no one. His parents had died in a plane crash when he was eighteen, then earlier this year, his brother Nico's body was found on the back step of The Laughing Loaf, a victim of poisoning.

"After our parents died, I wanted to get closer with Nico," Nate continued, looking down into the fire. "So I thought—let's do what we did when our parents were alive. It worked before, right? We went backpacking a few times, a few hikes into Angeles National Forest. It wasn't the same. Nico hated it. He kept asking if we could go to the outlet malls on the way back. He wanted to shop."

"You tried." I squeezed his hand. "You took your job as his guardian seriously." Nico hadn't made that easy for Nate. He'd been in and out of trouble since he was a teenager. His final plunge into trouble had cost him his life.

Nate gazed into the fire. "It didn't do any good."

"Sometimes the only reward for doing the right thing is knowing you did the right thing."

When I'd turned my ex-husband Ben in for selling defense secrets to foreign governments, it was the right thing to do. For my country—and for *me* since I didn't want to be caught up in his scheme. After testifying in court, I was immediately relocated to River Grove with my father and my dog, for our protection. I wasn't sure when someone from Russia, China, or North Korea would show up, looking for revenge or more secrets. I was still paying the price.

Nate turned to me quickly, a look of understanding on his face, the corner of his mouth turned up slightly. "You're right."

You'd think this would be a nice segue way into a conversation about why he'd called me my pre-witness protection name, *Grace*, on our drive from the airport back in October. I had been wondering lately: maybe he'd just said it because he assumed Gracie was a nickname for Grace.

But I wavered. When you're huddled together with someone you're very attracted to, the last thing you want to do is bring up something difficult or problematic.

I felt peaceful and happy right now, far away from the stresses of running my business, which hopefully was doing fine in Beck's capable hands.

So I said nothing.

Chapter Four

Saturday, December 7

Nate got up at 6 a.m. He was trying to keep quiet and not wake me, but I'm a light sleeper and I heard every carefully placed footstep.

I heard him rummaging through his camera bag, then zipping it up, prepping for his coastal shoot this morning.

In a few minutes, the smells of brewing coffee and bacon drifted in from the kitchen. The combination of those two smells was one of my favorite things.

I wandered in, my hair in bedhead mode, robe pulled around me.

"I thought breakfast would get you out of bed." He laughed at my tousled head as he set plates out on the dining table, which was next to a picture window with a view of the backyard and the deck. Nate poured each of us coffee from the drip maker.

The sun had come out, revealing a green field of grass beyond the backyard. Something furry was nosing around at the edge of the deck. Nate could probably identify it. It looked harmless enough, or at least I hoped it was.

Nate pulled a tray of bacon out of the oven and stacked slices on a plate with a pair of tongs.

I've always made food for everyone else. My ex-husband Ben feigned ignorance of the basics of food preparation, so I did everything. It's hard to exaggerate how amazing it felt to have someone cook for me.

It made me feel like a princess. It made my heart melt.

If I were a picky person, it might be different. I could get judgy about the food quality—this is not how I would make it. But Nate was a good cook, and he cleaned up after himself.

I reached up and threw my arms around his neck.

"Whoa—" He laughed and bent down (since there was almost a foot difference between us) and we leaned back against the butcher block and kissed, but not too long. The bacon was getting cold. "Now why do I deserve this?"

"You made me breakfast."

He slid into the seat across from me and passed me a plate of sliced ancient grain pumpkin bread from Night Rose. "It was my pleasure. And so was that." He grinned.

"I'm looking forward to what I can learn at Night Rose this morning," I said, as I slathered the European butter we'd picked up at the grocery store over the bread. I bit into it. The butter, with the nutty, spicy flavor of the bread, was delicious.

"Learn how to make that bread. I've already had one slice." Nate held his hands up. "I needed to stop there."

"I probably should, too," I said reluctantly, suspecting Nate had more self-control than I did. After the pumpkin bread, I finished off two slices of bacon, then on second thought, grabbed a third. I took a bite and sighed with pleasure. It was sweet, smoky and spicy at the same time.

"What's on the bacon?"

"Honey, black pepper and a dash of cinnamon."

"I had three pieces of it." I shook my head. "I don't remember deciding to eat it. It just jumped into my mouth."

"My college roommates taught me how to make it," he said as he got up to pour each of us another cup of coffee. "They called it Millionaire's Bacon."

As I sipped my coffee, I thought about what we saw at Night Rose yesterday. And I began to wonder whether inviting Daniel to teach at The Laughing Loaf had been a good idea.

"I hope Daniel behaves himself today. He's definitely got issues with his employees. From what I read in his book, he didn't get along with his co-owner at his last bakery. It sounds like there were lawyers involved."

"A familiar story." Nate raised his eyebrows as he took a sip of coffee. "Someone who's a genius but not so great with human beings."

"Everyone wants to work for Daniel because of his culinary reputation. Putting up with a narcissist could be worth it if you get good experience out of it."

"You do what you have to do when you're starting out." Nate nodded. "I had some harsh mentors. Brilliant photographers. Their comments could be soul crushing, but I knew it wouldn't last forever. I learned all I could from them, then moved on."

After we finished, Nate rinsed plates and cups and loaded the dishwasher, while I showered and combed through my wet hair to get it to calm down. I put on my nice jeans, walking boots, and a thick, warm wool sweater.

Nate would drive me to Night Rose, then continue down the road to Bodega Bay to shoot photos of a quirky seabird called a *guillemot*, a black bird with white feathers and bright red legs. It looked like a very vivid duck.

I could tell now when Nate was excited about work. He had this way of walking, of almost bouncing on his feet. A slight smile came over his face as if he were mulling over his secret gameplan for the shoot.

Night Rose was on the way to the coast. It was cold and foggy when Nate dropped me off. The area around the large barn structure looked desolate, except for a few people huddled in a clump near the door. The picnic tables were all empty. It was a few minutes before 7 a.m.

I approached the group waiting near the door. There were two very clean-shaven guys a little younger than me, holding cups of coffee. A lanky man a little older than me wore a long, white linen tunic and a bandana tied around his head. He looked like he could have belonged to Reggie McFerrin's original River Grove hippie commune. There was an older guy near retirement age whose muscular forearms looked like he spent a lot of time kneading dough.

"You're all here for the class with Daniel?"

Nods around the group.

I pressed my face against the window in the bakery's front door.

"It looks dark in there. Is Daniel even here?"

As soon as I said that, I heard angry voices coming from inside--upstairs, from the sound of it. I pulled closer, trying to figure out who might be talking and what they were saying. One of them I recognized as Daniel. The other sounded like a woman. The yelling escalated to screams. Then a door slammed.

"I didn't think anyone was in there till I heard the yelling," bandana man said with concern in his voice. "I've been here for fifteen minutes."

One of the young guys looked into the window near the door. "The counter and baking area look empty."

"Maybe he's upstairs. He could be running late." I pulled out my phone to check for any notifications, since I'd registered for the class with my phone number at the bakery yesterday. "I don't have any texts about it."

"I'm surprised no one's working in the baking area," the older guy said. "Bakery work starts early in the morning."

"I come in at 4:30 a.m.," I said with a nod. "And my operation's a lot smaller than Night Rose."

Bandana man turned to me. "What bakery?"

"The Laughing Loaf. We're in River Grove, in the Santa Cruz Mountains."

"My name's Koa Wilson. I own a bakery up in Eureka," he said. "Moonbeams. We're entirely vegan. We're thinking of renovating the woodfired oven that came with the place."

"I'm Gracie Markley." I smiled and held out my hand. "I'm interested in seeing what a woodfired oven can do. As we grow, we might want to invest in one."

We talked for a while in the group, shivering as we introduced ourselves, until a young woman with red hair came over from the parking lot. I immediately recognized her: Maeve, from the register, the one Daniel had threatened yesterday.

"Why aren't you all inside?" She looked at us, startled. "You're here for the woodfired demonstration, right?"

"We heard a lot of yelling," Koa told the young woman. "Other than that, it looks deserted inside."

Maeve looked at the door. She frowned but didn't look surprised.

She pulled a ring of keys from her purse and opened the bakery door. She walked inside. Though most of our little group looked uneasy about entering, Koa and I looked at each other and followed Maeve in.

The place was empty and cold. Maeve began to switch on lights.

"Daniel must be here," she said, her voice echoing in the cavernous stillness. "His car's in the lot. We were short-handed yesterday. He was pretty angry about it." She blew out her breath and glanced around the room. Tables were clean and tidy. Floors were swept. Just like Beck left things when she closed up The Laughing Loaf. With the level of intimidation he apparently used on his workers, I'm sure the Night Rose staff made sure everything was up to Daniel's standards at the end of the day.

Maeve stood and thought for a moment, tapping her lips with her finger.

"Looks like he's started up the ovens. Let me check his office."

Maeve headed up the wooden stairs at the back of the bakery.

Koa looked very impatient. "He probably blew us off."

"This doesn't seem like something he'd do," I said. "He's a professional."

"Really?" Koa was skeptical. "He's also a real hothead. He probably got mad at his staff and blew them off. He's off having a temper tantrum somewhere."

"He has his moods, from what I've heard," I said, wondering if Koa had anger issues or was just tired from the long drive down from Eureka. "But I can't see him having time to do that. He's got a bakery to run."

A minute later, I backed out of the way as a young blonde woman headed past us for the door, her lips twisted into a pout. She gave Koa and me a look of surprise, then opened the door and barreled through it. Through the window, I watched her stomp off to the parking lot beyond the picnic tables.

Finally, at 7:25 a.m., Daniel Bordleman came downstairs and met us at the counter. He looked exhausted this morning, shadowy circles under his eyes, but a rosy glow to his face. He looked us over, then grunted at us.

"Let's meet at the far end. Line up at the middle row tables."

The rest of the group from outside shuffled into the bakery, and Rafal from yesterday opened the low gate for us. We settled into spots at the tables. Daniel stood near the ovens and addressed us.

"The purpose of this demonstration is for you to see how different it is to bake bread in a woodfired oven. If you've been using a conventional oven, get used to the fact that nothing is dialed in here." Daniel looked at all of us sternly. "You need to keep an eye on the temperature and control it. The ideal air temperature in the oven before baking should be 480-500 degrees Fahrenheit, and that will go down as soon as you put in your loaf. If you control your temperature and make sure you have the right amount of humidity, you'll get a beautiful, crisp crust and an inside that's soft. If you can't control these variables, your loaf is worthless."

Rafal had cut a large mound of dough into small portions and laid a dough ball in front of each of us. I dusted mine with flour and began pressing down and shaping it to form a tight boule for baking.

Over at the counter, I saw Maeve tie on her Night Rose apron, preparing for her workday. She threw a grim look in Rafal's direction, and their eyes connected.

Something felt off this morning. The atmosphere felt tense, as if it would shatter with a wrong move or dropped utensil. Maybe this was just a normal day at Night Rose. All

I knew was this bakery had a very different vibe than The Laughing Loaf.

And it wasn't a happy one.

After we'd formed our boules, Daniel taught us how to slide them into the oven on the peel by giving the peel a jerk and a push. The boule slid onto the floor of the hot oven. One of my favorite things about bread-making is the magical transformation from dough to a crusty, finished loaf. I looked forward to seeing what my boule would look like.

When I slid the peel under the boule and brought it out fifteen minutes later, the bread was dark brown and crusty, rustic and beautiful.

"Why does it have to be so dark?" One of the young guys asked. "It looks burned."

"Do you not even understand the Maillard Reaction?" Daniel said with scorn in his voice. "Would you eat a pale, boiled steak? Of course not—you want some char, some color on it. The effects of heat make the crust a culinary delight. With the intense heat, the sugars and protein are transformed, creating a richer flavor and smell." He bent down over my boule on the cooling rack, fresh out of the oven, and took a deep breath. He closed his eyes in ecstasy.

"That's it. That's what you want. It enchants the senses."

I'd had dark-crusted bread like this in Paris. I remembered savoring the depth of flavor and crunchy texture, the results of the Maillard Reaction.

Someday, I would get one of these ovens for The Laughing Loaf.

After the demonstration had finished, Maeve opened the front door of the bakery, and Night Rose was open for business. Those who had taken the class with me lingered to talk. The two young guys seemed unimpressed with their darkened bread. They set them on the table and left.

Koa told me he was going back to Eureka to have the old woodfired oven in Moonbeams Bakery restored and ready for service.

"Nothing compares to that flavor."

I flagged down Daniel.

"That was a great demonstration. Got a few minutes to talk about the class at the Laughing Loaf?"

Daniel sighed heavily, then looked around at the remaining students, who were hovering over their bread rounds, waiting for them to cool so they could sample them. I know bakers need to get up long before anyone else, but he looked like he'd been up all night. He badly needed a shave and probably a shower. He waved at me distractedly then rubbed his eyes with his palm.

"Come up to the video room. Let's talk."

Upstairs, Daniel slid wearily into the chair behind his desk. "Fine. Show me your bakery."

I pulled out my phone and showed him photos of the back room at The Laughing Loaf, and photos of the stately 1900s former bank building and River Grove's old school downtown.

He nodded, as he propped up his chin on his arm, looking half bored. "Sure. I'm digging the vibe. Very photogenic. That'll work. Who's the girl?"

I got a little defensive, my big-sister-bear hackles rising at him calling my star employee "the girl." "That's Beck. She's my assistant manager."

"She'd be great for the video. I'll bring her a costume."

Beck would absolutely love this. "She's crazy about your videos. I'll ask her today, but she'll probably be thrilled to be part of it."

Daniel Bordleman sat back in his chair, bleary eyed. "I get into town Friday afternoon. Maybe we can shoot then. We'll do a two-hour class on Saturday morning. I'll cover starter and a basic sourdough recipe. Then we come back to bake on Sunday morning."

"That can work. I can arrange help that day, so we should be okay." I smiled. "I think this can work out well for both of us, Daniel."

There was a bitter look on his face. I didn't take it personally, since it looked like he was still mulling over whatever had happened between him and the blonde woman before our class.

He grimaced as he handed me my phone and grunted.

"Well, it *better*."

Chapter Five

Nate wasn't swinging by to pick me up till 11 a.m., so I ordered a breakfast scone and pourover coffee from Maeve and took it outside to the picnic tables. I sat down and texted Beck the unbelievably good news: Daniel Bordleman was coming to The Laughing Loaf to teach a sourdough class next weekend. And he wanted her to be in a video.

A few minutes later I received a text from Beck - a happy face, followed by about twenty hearts and a series of exclamation points.

I laughed out loud. I was eager to know how Beck was doing with Chloe and Aiden and Winter Pastry Fest. I hadn't gotten any desperate calls.

> So tell me...How's it going?

Beck responded with a series of thumbs-up emojis and a heart.

Why did I ask? If she was having some problems at the

bakery—apart from it burning down— she wouldn't interrupt my getaway anyway.

It was a chilly morning, so I pulled my sweater up around my neck and looked across the street at the cows grazing in their bright green pasture. I wrapped my hands around my coffee to warm them.

In a few minutes, Maeve came out with a coffee, saw me, and took a seat at the picnic table, across from me. Her face had a pinched look.

"On break?"

She took a sip and frowned. "I had to get out for just a few. I'm ready to punch Daniel in the face. Carina's covering for me."

"He's in a bad mood today?"

Maeve rolled her eyes. "Not just today." She shook her head and looked down at the table. "After you work here a while, you see he's that way with all his employees. Well— except Ashley."

Despite what Nate had said about the rewards of learning from a bad mentor, I shook my head. Why should anyone have to put up with this?

"Daniel is very kind to customers. He yells at us one moment then turns around and is the nicest guy ever to somebody in line. His philosophy is, 'Be nice to the customers. They're responsible for your paycheck.'"

Granted, Daniel was a jerk. As a business owner, though, I knew that the paycheck statement was true. Good customer service was a huge part of a business's success.

"If he's so bad, why are you still here?" I asked, puzzled.

Maeve took a sip of her coffee. "This is one of the best bakeries in California. I'm learning about bread here. It might kill me, but I'll put up with Daniel for a while longer."

I wondered why she'd stay on to learn at such a cost if she wasn't even involved in the breadmaking.

"Maeve, you're just working the counter, aren't you?"

She groaned in frustration. "Daniel refuses to let me learn in the baking room." She lowered her voice and leaned toward me. "So Rafal is teaching me. After everybody goes home. He's been teaching me for the past year and a half. If Daniel knew, he'd be furious. But I'm learning so much." Her lightly freckled face glowed for a moment. "Daniel tries to put Rafal down, to try to keep him in his place. He picks on things like Rafal's knife skills because he can't fault him on his baking. Rafal's a great baker. He's helped make this bakery famous."

I took a Laughing Loaf business card out of my purse and handed it to her. Who knew? She might need a job someday. We definitely needed help at The Laughing Loaf.

She took the card and looked it over gratefully. "Thanks, Gracie."

"Maeve," I said in the same low voice. "This morning before you came, a blonde woman was having an argument upstairs with Daniel. A screaming match. She stomped out, right before you got there."

Maeve looked amused. "That's Ashley. Ashley Fontaine, the assistant manager. If she's mad at Daniel —wow."

I gave her a quizzical look. "Why do you say that?"

"She's the Chosen One. She can do no wrong in Daniel's eyes. For us employees, she's the same as Daniel, as far as how badly she treats us. She learned it all from him." She raised her eyebrows and took a sip of coffee.

"Oh, yeah. And they're *married*."

* * *

After Nate picked me up, we drove back to the farmhouse.

I laid on the bed for almost an hour, but I couldn't nap. I couldn't stop thinking about my conversation with Maeve at the picnic table. I loved so much about Night Rose—its baked goods with their unusual flavor combos, its woodfired ovens, its sandwiches. The beautiful location in the Sonoma countryside. But the more time I spent there, the more I saw that its owner was a cruel and intimidating human being.

At 2:15 p.m., my phone vibrated with a text from a local phone number.

> This is Maeve. Daniel just fired Rafal. He left before I could talk to him.

> I'm worried about him.

> Gracie, could I visit your bakery sometime?

Was it right to invite Daniel to my bakery and let him teach a two-day class?

On the other hand, he was a world-class baker. He'd bring star power to my little bakery. Beck and I could both learn from his skills. It could be a great opportunity.

I opened my laptop. I searched for the man's video channel.

I clicked on the one that focused on Night Rose's havarti, dill, and pastrami sandwiches. Judging by the video's comment section, they'd been a favorite for a long time.

Like all his videos, this one opened with Daniel, a light shining down on his wide-eyed face, in a dark, empty kitchen. Mysterious music played. The camera pulled back and the lights went on, to reveal a bread table set up with the flours and ingredients for the bread he was making.

"Here's our yeast," he explained. "Add a little warm water and a teaspoon of sugar to the bowl to feed these ravenous creatures. Then let it sit." He clapped his hands and thanks to the magic of film editing, the yeast was suddenly frothy. "Look at it!" He proclaimed dramatically. "It's *alive*... and it is very happy."

"Today we're making rye bread with dill and havarti. Rye can be a *frightening* bread to attempt, but I'll show you how you can mix flours with higher gluten content in with the rye flour to get it to rise...*from the dead!*"

Daniel added dark rye flour to the stand mixer, then poured in some high-gluten flour and all-purpose flour.

Nate came in and lay down next to me as I watched, just as Daniel blended grated havarti and fresh dill into the mix.

"This is the bread we ate yesterday in our sandwiches," Nate said excitedly, as he started watching with me.

Daniel clapped his hands, which caused the dough to suddenly rise high in the plastic tub—through the magic of stop-motion video. Then he floured the table and used a bench scraper to cut the light brown dough into loaves and set them in pans to rise. I loved rye bread and hadn't included it in The Laughing Loaf's offerings in a while. I could practically smell the bread we'd eaten in our sandwiches yesterday as I watched Daniel slide the pans into the oven. I'd have to include rye in our rotation at the bakery. It wasn't one of our most popular breads, but the people who liked rye *really* liked it. I still got requests for it after making a batch of it a year ago.

I stopped the video and exited YouTube.

"He's pretty entertaining," Nate laughed. "Very over-the-top."

"Now that I found out from one of his workers what a jerk he is, I almost regret inviting him to do the class at The Laughing Loaf."

Nate leaned his head on his elbow and gazed at me with his baby blues. He was looking adorable. "He's only mean to his employees because they're his. He probably won't do that at The Laughing Loaf."

"He *better* not," I spat out.

"So he teaches his class, then he goes away. You don't have to see him again."

I turned toward him on the bed. "I guess it's a one-time thing. Beck and I will learn a lot. And anyone else who comes to the class."

"Gracie, this is your business, not mine." Nate reached out to hold my hand. "But Daniel runs a big bakery. The Laughing Loaf is growing. You're bringing in customers from out of the area now. He might be helpful in showing you how you can grow. He could be a mentor for that."

I had actually thought of that, but I was also afraid of growth. The Laughing Loaf was my happy place. A quiet, safe part of my life in River Grove.

"Let's have some lunch," he bent over and kissed me lightly. "Then how about a hike? The coast is only twenty minutes away."

Fresh air and crashing waves sounded like what I needed right now.

I closed my laptop. "Let's do it."

* * *

After devouring a really good sandwich made from Nate's leftover tri-tip, I put on my hiking boots, and we drove out to Highway 1, to Bodega Bay.

Nate left his camera bag at the house, being his boy scout self and trying to abide by our original pledge not to do work. I'd done a bad job of holding up my end of that deal.

As we parked the car, I remembered the old movie, *The Birds*, which was filmed here in the small town of Bodega Bay.

"You've seen the Hitchcock movie, right?" I remembered watching it with some friends in high school. The movie's slow-burn suspense and creepy images of birds going postal terrified us. And we loved it.

Nate grinned. "Anti-bird propaganda. Don't believe any of it. I had no problem with the birds this morning. No attacks, no slow gathering of birds behind me as I took my shots."

Since it was heading into mid-afternoon, we decided to take a shorter trail – a four-mile loop on the peninsula on the western side of Bodega Bay. It was overcast but ruggedly beautiful.

We walked along hills overlooking the ocean, then went further inland to see fields of grass and more birds. Nate's eyes lit up. He excitedly pointed out the different kinds to me. He'd left his camera behind but not his binoculars, and he knew what to look for. In among the grasses, and in nests in the trees, we saw some beautiful birds most people wouldn't see hiking the trail.

From what I'd seen of California, the further north you go, the colder and rockier the beaches get. Southern California beaches feel sandy and tropical, ideal for sunbathing. Santa Cruz, where River Grovians went when they wanted a legit ocean beach and not just the riverbank, was colder and foggier but still fine for sunbathing and volleyball. The Sonoma coast was a change from all that: cold, overcast, moody, and rocky. Not a comfortable place to lay out your beach towel, but it had a striking beauty. We stood for several minutes on the trail, looking down at the endless expanse of the Pacific Ocean.

"I feel small." Nate squeezed my hand as he towered over me. "It goes on forever."

"When I was little, we sometimes took drives out to the Washington coast, to the Olympic Peninsula. I remember my mother telling me that just across the ocean was Japan. Every time we went, I'd look out and squint my eyes, thinking that if I just focused hard enough, I could see Japan. I never could."

Nate bent down to kiss my head. "You must have been very disappointed."

"I was *very* disappointed." I laughed. "Then my dad would launch into a long scientific explanation that involved the curvature of the earth and how far away Japan really was. There was no way I'd be able to see it. Talk about a downer."

"I can hear the lecture now." Nate chuckled.

This afternoon, it felt good to be outdoors, with no schedule or agenda.

I dreaded telling Beck that the YouTube sourdough baker she'd come to love was not such a great guy. Though I would take her aside and talk to her before our weekend class with Daniel.

I was dying to know how Winter Pastry Fest was going at The Laughing Loaf. Hopefully the day had gone smoothly, with lots of customers but not overwhelming crowds. Right now, Beck, Chloe and Aiden would be cleaning up and getting everything ready for the next day's bakes.

I'm sure she'd dealt with some challenges—I did in any given workday—but Beck was a resourceful young woman and would figure out how to handle them.

I hoped.

Chapter Six

After our hike on Bodega Head, we drove along Bay Flat Road, joining up with Highway 1, which was lined with restaurants, souvenir shops and a visitor center.

We found a fish market and parked in its lot to check out their selection of fresh-caught fish. We looked over their display case full of salmon, halibut, and crab. The smell and offerings reminded me of Pike Place Market in Seattle, a familiar place to me. I had to remind myself not to bring it up because, according to my witness protection bio, I was supposed to be from Portland, not Seattle, and I'd already given Nate a short version of that story.

Nate was excited about trying fresh oysters, which I had zero interest in. They looked slimy and gelatinous—not something I wanted to put into my body. The man at the counter brought one out for him. Nate tipped the shell, downed the oyster, and grinned.

I'd wait a while before I kissed him again.

We were standing by the display counter when a man in a jacket, his cap pulled down to his eyebrows and his hands in his pockets, walked into the shop and started looking at a display of sourdough bread and cheeses. Nate turned and watched the man as he looked over the bags of bread.

"I think that's the baker from Night Rose," he pulled close to me and whispered. "Rafal."

I dashed toward the door. Rafal saw me and turned to flee into the parking lot. I took off, slowly gaining on him. Suddenly he looked back, saw me coming after him, and broke into a sprint.

"Rafal! Wait."

Soon Nate, whose legs were a lot longer than mine, dashed out of the store and took off after the baker. I saw, in the distance, that Nate had caught up with him. Whatever Nate had said to him had made him stop. They stood talking as Rafal bent over to catch his breath. Slowly they walked back towards the shop.

I jog-walked until I got to the two men. Rafal's dark eyes looked me over nervously.

"Rafal, I only wanted to talk to you." I noticed the young man's eyes were red rimmed. His lip was twisted in anger. He looked like he didn't want to talk and was waiting for us to leave him alone.

"You two—I saw you go upstairs at the bakery with Daniel. You're his friends. That's why I ran."

I shook my head. "We aren't his friends. That was the first time I'd met Daniel. Maeve told me this morning that Daniel fired you."

Rafal looked down at his feet. "I was teaching her at night. Daniel threatened to fire her if she did it, but to be honest—I never thought he'd fire *me*."

Nate didn't get angry very often, but I could see his face tense up, his nostrils flaring as he shook his head.

"Maeve said you left before she could talk to you. She's worried about you."

Rafal's eyes softened and a corner of his mouth turned up. "She is?"

He led us behind the shop, to a table that overlooked the bay.

Nate and I sat down while Rafal took a seat across from us. Rafal flexed his hands, his face red with anger.

"My life is over." He shook his head. "I don't have a job. I can't pay my rent. I may not be able to stay in the country. After all I did for Night Rose, I can't believe he fired me."

"How long had you worked at the bakery?" I asked him.

"Six years. I learned a lot from him, but I also helped him build his business. The job was my life. He's one of the worst people I've ever worked for."

I raised my eyebrows. That was pretty clear.

"What will you do now?" Nate asked him.

"Look for any work I can get. I have the experience at Night Rose. But everyone in Sonoma knows Daniel. It's his word against mine, and he just told me what a horrible baker and employee I am. My chances aren't good."

I pulled a Laughing Loaf business card out of my bag and handed it to him.

"My bakery needs help from time to time. I can't guarantee anything long-term, but Laughing Loaf is growing. And I know some bakers in the South Bay. I'll keep my ears open. If I hear of any opportunities, I'll let you know."

"Thank you," Rafal said, but anger still simmered in his eyes. He stood up and pulled his cap down lower over his head. "This is my problem. I'll have to deal with it my way."

"Hey, man." Nate pulled a bill out of his pocket and slipped it to Rafal, palm to palm, in an offhand and casual way. Rafal nodded, looking grateful and embarrassed at the same time.

Nate and I watched Rafal walk away then get into a battered compact car in the parking lot.

Maybe the sourdough class would be a good thing, but after talking to Rafal, I felt even worse about the idea of Daniel Bordleman setting foot in my bakery.

Chapter Seven

That evening was the last night of our getaway.

We'd decided to go out to eat instead of cooking at the hut.

As Nate and I sat down to a romantic dinner at a winery in Napa, I vowed to put thoughts of Daniel Bordleman, Rafal, and Night Rose out of my head. I wanted to drink really good wine, eat food prepared by someone else, and be fully with Nate.

A bank of windows in the dining room looked out onto the vineyard, and lights hung along the rows, highlighting the vines in the darkness as they stretched out into the distance. To the side of the window, a jazz combo played instrumental music. I looked across the table at Nate, dressed in his classic going-out look: a button-down vest over a crisp white shirt, and nice jeans. His dark hair was pulled back into a short, neat ponytail. When the candle on the table reflected in his eyes, my heart thumped along with the standup bass.

"So much for not doing work on this trip." I took a generous sip of pinot noir and reached out for his hand. "I'm sorry to drag you into the Night Rose mess. I didn't know any of that was going to happen."

"We've had two great days together. Life with you is not boring. And it usually involves bread." A corner of his mouth turned up in a crooked smile. "How can I complain about that?"

"Thanks." My voice sounded overly quiet, faint as a whisper.

I wanted to ask him. *Why did you call me Grace when I picked you up from the airport back in October? If you know about my past, tell me. Then I'll be able to relax.*

But the way his eyes were shining at me, I couldn't.

After our dinner, we walked out of the front entrance into the cool air, where two of the band members were taking their break at the edge of the parking lot. A guitarist and a violinist. As musicians who enjoy playing together do, they used the time out to continue jamming. We stood listening for a while in the cool, clear night air as they played jazz standards, then their own renditions of some pop songs.

Nate reached for my hand and pulled me toward him. I wasn't a dancer by any means, but he was good at it, and it was an invitation I wasn't going to refuse. He spun me around and I let myself follow him, falling into the rhythm as we clasped hands together and danced, old-person style, in the parking lot near the restaurant's entrance. My arms, my legs, and my mind felt light and free. It felt natural and easy to dance with him.

The band continued playing as they watched us. After conferring with each other with a few words and a nod, the two musicians picked up the tempo to play an all-strings version of a Guns and Roses song.

When we finished, the band stopped playing and clapped for us. Nate grinned and gave me a kiss.

As we drove back to our hut, I lay back against the seat, content.

"So how do you know how to do that?"

He glanced over at me. "What, the dancing?"

"Granted, I'm not good at it at all. But you actually know what you're doing."

Nate laughed. "I went to a high school where ballroom dancing was a mandatory part of PE. At the time, all I thought was how embarrassing it was to be forced to dance with a bunch of other 14-year-olds. But I learned how to do it. Valuable life skill achieved."

I raised my eyebrows and smiled.

"You have many secrets, Nate."

He paused for a moment, as we pulled onto Bodega Highway. I could see him looking at me in the darkness.

"You do, too," he said, in a way that suddenly paralyzed me.

What could I say to that? Spill all the info about Ben, my court testimony, and my witness protection relocation?

"There are things I wish I could tell you, Nate. I'm not the kind of person who likes secrets—or who gets any joy from withholding information."

After pulling into the driveway, he stopped the car and turned to me, his face still shrouded in the darkness.

The porch light lit up his face. I saw him frown, his face serious.

"Yeah. I'm getting that."

* * *

SUNDAY, *December 8*

Our drive back to River Grove the next morning seemed uncomfortably quiet.

Nate and I did companionable silence well; neither of us had ever felt the need to fill the space with small talk when we were together. So it was probably just my anxiety creeping up. I'd drawn the line last night with what I could tell him. Maybe it had confirmed some things for him.

Did he know I was in witness protection? Now I wanted to know what he'd been thinking about our conversation. He seemed to be quieter after we'd talked last night.

"You okay?" I looked across at him.

"Yeah. Fine." He didn't turn to me, just looked straight ahead.

I don't think it was my imagination. Nate had been withdrawn on our drive back, and I was uneasy about what would come next.

Nate drove quickly, traffic was light, and we ended up back in River Grove by 2 p.m. Nate helped me carry my bags into the house, then when I walked with him out to the front porch, he gave me a decent kiss. He said goodbye, looking serious and thoughtful.

Nice kiss. So we're good, right?

Or not.

I wasn't sure.

I breathed a sigh of relief that Mary Jo wasn't there at the house. Though I did notice a few leftovers in the fridge, which probably came from their cooking collaborations while we were gone.

My father came out of his study to greet us, rubbing his eyes. He looked like he'd just woken up.

"Where is Nate?" My father looked around the room. Then Biga came out of my room. He started trembling —*Can it be? Is she really back?*—then ran to me. I picked him up and rubbed my face against the smooth fur on his head.

"Nate left." My bottom lip trembled a bit. I pressed my lips together, trying to control it. "Had to get home."

"How was it?" My father asked me.

I felt uneasy, as sadness washed over me.

"It was—good," I said haltingly. I mean, it had been great up until our conversation driving back from the restaurant last night.

Untypically, my father came over and hugged me. His embrace set loose the tears clogging my throat. I felt like a five-year-old who'd crashed her bike and skinned her knee.

I was glad he'd asked. He led me to the kitchen table and pulled out a chair. I held Biga close, and my little dog began licking my face, which made me tear up again.

"Let me pour you a cuppa, dear." My father went to the stove and started up the tea kettle. "Then why don't you tell me exactly what happened."

Chapter Eight

After my cup of tea and a short nap, I decided to pull myself together and get over to the Laughing Loaf to prep for tomorrow and hear from Beck how the Winter Pastry Fest went.

After my confusing time with Nate, I looked forward to being back in my familiar routine. At the bakery, I knew what I had to do. I knew how to make bread. I knew how to bake things, and I did it well. The rhythms, cycles, and routines of the bakery would anchor me. I would not have to think.

As I approached the back door, I heard the familiar thump of music. Then soon, Beck's light, girlish voice earnestly singing along with Adam Ant's "Goody Two Shoes," a song from before her time, and mine.

When I opened the door, I heard her shriek with glee.

"Gracie! Oh my God, you're back." She turned from her spot at the metal table, where she was cutting a rectangle of rolled-out beignet dough, and ran over to give me a hug, floured hands and all. "I didn't think you'd be in till later."

I shrugged. "I had to hear how it went. And I missed the place, after spending time at someone else's bakery."

She laughed, nudging her errant chef hat back onto her head with the side of her arm. "I want to hear all about it. I can't believe you got Daniel Bordleman to come teach a class at The Laughing Loaf! And he's going to make one of his videos here. And you said I get to be in it—is this for real? I can't wait!"

I grimaced. I hated to burst Beck's image of her video idol. "Well, there are a few things I learned about Daniel that you should know. But we can talk about that later. Tell me how things went with the pastry fest. Be honest. I want to hear everything. Even the mistakes."

I looked around the back room, then went out into the dining area. Beck followed me up to the front. Every surface was spotless.

Beck laughed, a little nervously. "It wasn't perfect. I burned a days' worth of tarts because I needed to help Chloe with a problem with the cinnamon rolls she was making. I had to toss all the apple tarts, so we didn't have any yesterday. Some people were mad about that."

She groaned in frustration. "And Aiden didn't show up on Saturday till 10 a.m.—right when were super busy—because he slept in. We had to have *my* mom call *his* mom so she could leave her job at the bank and go wake him up. So Chloe and I had a tough time managing the back room and the counter until he got here. There were a few really impatient customers."

"That's tough, Beck." I let out a sigh of relief. "But if that's the worst of it, that's really not that bad."

She brightened. "It felt bad at the time, but we survived it."

"What did you feel best about from the Pastry Fest?"

Beck smiled. "Everyone in town was happy that we were doing it. Everyone came in, excited to buy sweets. We sold out of all our beignets every day in the first hour. Chloe counted—we had 73 customers Friday, the first day. Then 96 on Saturday, and 89 today."

My mouth gaped open. This was an incredible turnout. But we had promoted the fest for a good three weeks, and River Grove was a town with a pretty serious sweet tooth.

I put on my Laughing Loaf apron and went to wash my hands. I'd start mixing bread doughs, so we could go back to offering loaves tomorrow.

"Thank you for all you did, Beck." I pulled out the mixing tubs and turned on the proofer. "I can't tell you how good it felt to get away and not have to worry about the bakery. I knew it was in good hands."

Beck blushed, and she smiled shyly.

"I can't wait till I learn about baking bread, so I can help more with that."

I sighed under my breath as I eyeballed two cups of sourdough starter and scooped it into a tub. I would need to prepare Beck for the fact that her celebrity crush wasn't a great guy after all.

"Yeah, we should talk about that. It was great to visit Night Rose. They had some of the best bread I've ever had, and Daniel is a brilliant baker. But there are some downsides to him. I want to set this class up and make sure it's a good experience for everyone. And that the video shoot is a good experience for you, Beck."

Beck looked puzzled, but she nodded.

"I'm doing a Zoom with Daniel about the setup for the class tomorrow afternoon. We have a lot to pull together by the weekend. When we get a break mid-morning, I want to brainstorm some ideas with you."

"That sounds great!"

The excitement and sheer joy on her face suddenly made me wish I could also look forward to Saturday's class —without knowing all I'd learned on my getaway.

Beck stayed to finish the tart shells and beignet dough, and in the closed bakery, we played music, sang loudly and danced around the room as we moved between our baking projects. It felt so good to be back at The Laughing Loaf again. Thoughts of Nate entered my mind, but I didn't dwell on them. There was always something else to prep. After mixing dough for tomorrow, I tidied my office, then I ordered rye flour, with the idea of recreating the delicious rye havarti bread at Night Rose.

Maybe Nate had been right in his suggestion that I could learn from Daniel Bordleman as The Laughing Loaf grew. For the past month, I'd been trying to accept that my business was doing well—and that wasn't a bad thing. I was bringing in customers from the coast and from Silicon Valley now. Did I need to worry that this would bring in foreign agents? If foreign agents wanted to find me, they would, whether or not my business was well known.

Daniel was a jerk. I thought about what Nate had said about learning valuable skills from even the worst teachers.

I could learn from the *Night of the Living Bread* baker, but I didn't have to be like him. And though he'd texted me that he'd booked an Airbnb in the hills for his stay, his time in town would actually be short. Just two sessions, one on a Saturday, one on a Sunday. If he treated Beck or anyone else badly, I'd take him aside.

The weekend class and the video could do a lot for The Laughing Loaf. I wanted to learn all I could, then send Daniel Bordleman on his way.

After Beck left for the day, I printed out a registration

form then added a blurb about the class to The Laughing Loaf website.

I thought of who to invite. Since Daniel was hoping to create some promotional buzz with this class, I thought of Susan Federer, a food blogger from Santa Cruz who'd stopped by the bakery last month. And Marco, a YouTube reviewer who'd included The Laughing Loaf in a Bay Area bakery wrap-up. I texted them both.

Then I stayed at the bakery to experiment a bit. Night Rose's savory scones had impressed me as a great breakfast offering, and I wanted to play with some flavors.

I did have scallions, thyme and some dill in my fridge, so I pulled things out and did some chopping. I reduced the sugar in my standard scone recipe and folded in the chopped ingredients and some white cheddar, then did my laminating—sprinkling grated frozen butter over the top, then folding, turning and rolling out the dough each time to create a stack of layers.

I'd just slid two trays into the freezer, when I heard a knock on the front door. I ran to the front, where I saw Nate standing alongside his bike. Quickly, I unlocked the door. His face had the same seriousness he'd had earlier today. In fact, it had intensified. My stomach twisted uncomfortably.

"Gracie—may I come in for a minute?" His voice sounded very formal.

I opened the door and waved him in.

"When I got back into my studio, I saw I'd gotten an invitation to do a shoot in Oregon for a raptor refuge. It's a short assignment, but I decided to take some extra time up there. To think. I need to get outdoors." He cleared his throat.

"Nate, what's going on?" I tried to keep any note of a

whine from my voice. "Was it something from the trip? Please tell me."

He looked at me directly, but his eyes were soft.

"You know how I feel about you, Gracie. It wasn't the getaway. I just—I need to think some things through." He sighed. "I can't pretend everything's okay, when I'm still trying to figure out how our relationship would work long term. Believe me, it's not you." He looked at me intently, as if willing me to understand without him having to say it. "It's your situation."

My witness protection status. My stomach knotted even more. "Why can't we talk about it together?"

He shook his head and responded gruffly. "It's something I have to work through. Best place for me to do that is outdoors."

I gulped and took a deep breath. "Okay."

"I'll be back in about a week." He shifted on his feet and prepared to roll his bike back outside. We'd gotten so close on our getaway. I wanted to cry but didn't feel like I could.

He bent toward me, keeping his bike between us and gave me a kiss. A kiss you'd give your grandma.

On weak legs, I walked to the door and opened it for him. He rolled his bike out onto the sidewalk and looked at me one last time. Whatever had been going through his head was intense; he did not look happy. He looked like he'd fallen into a pit of deep thought and wasn't sure if he could climb back out.

"Goodbye, Nate."

After he took off down the street, I shut and locked the door.

I wanted to text Elana, but of course, we weren't friends anymore.

I paced through the renovated old bank building. I was in my bakery, with one of my biggest sources of comfort.

Baking had gotten me through my teen years. It had gotten me through the shock of what Ben had been doing behind my back.

I knew how this worked.

It was time to bake.

I went back to my scones on the metal table. I decided to bake a few of the ones I'd put into the freezer. They smelled amazing in the oven, a mélange of herbs, butter, and garlic. It came to me as I smelled the scones baking, that the cheddar wasn't quite right. I rooted through drawers in the industrial fridge and found some feta cheese, tangy and rich. I'd mix a new batch, also toning down the garlic.

I stayed another hour, splitting the dough into smaller batches and playing with combinations and proportions of herbs and cheese. The pursuit of the right flavor combo kept me focused. Then I plated them in groups and did a taste of each combo.

As it baked, the final batch smelled like a Mediterranean street market. I pulled out the tray and laid the scones out on the cooling rack, then went to organize the supply room, to keep myself from devouring the scones before they were ready.

When I finally pulled one off the cooling rack, I set it on a plate. I picked it up and took a bite off the end. I closed my eyes, enveloped by the flavors and smell. It was rich, fresh and comforting. Maybe I did have something in common with Daniel Bordleman and his obsession with new and unusual combinations of flavors.

The lamination had created buttery, flaky layers that melted in my mouth. The fresh herbs made me feel like I was walking through the woods after a rain, and the feta added a sharp bite of creaminess.

Whatever my dad wanted for dinner, I'd make it or order it for him. This would be my dinner. My distraction from my boyfriend heading out of town when I really wanted to be with him.

And it was perfect.

Chapter Nine

That night, I kept busy.

I challenged my dad to a game of chess and lost badly, as usual. I cuddled with Biga while I listened to a mystery audiobook, then I wrote up my list of questions for tomorrow's Zoom session with Daniel Bordleman.

When I fell asleep, I was out for the night—bundled and warm on a cold winter night under my heavy down comforter, Biga's warm little body wedged up next to me. I didn't wake up to ponder what Nate must be thinking about.

Nate wasn't my ex-husband Ben. I'd rather deal with Nate asking himself questions in the forest—than someone who tricked me and was ready to make me suffer for his crimes.

Nate said what he meant. Nate reminded me of WYSIWYG, an old term from the computer industry. It meant that something on the screen appeared just as it would look when you printed it—no codes or formatting language. What you see is what you get – WYSIWYG.

There was not a lot of hidden information with Nate. If he was angry, you could see it on his face. If he was feeling love for me, it beamed from his face or it came out in his actions.

Nate had gone off by himself to think about how to deal with my witness protection status.

I stared up at the bedroom ceiling, listening to drops of rain as they tapped on the roof.

* * *

MONDAY, *December 9*

Considering how disappointing Sunday had been, I woke up Monday morning feeling much better.

I shivered as I pulled clothes from the dryer and got dressed in the cold early morning. I got up earlier today--at 3:30 a.m. I wanted to give myself some time to plan for Daniel's class before Beck came in.

Biga jumped down off the bed, eager to go with me. After my time away, he wasn't about to let me out of his sight again. He made a beeline for his crate, sitting down next to it expectantly. This was not typical Biga behavior.

The high schoolers poured into the bakery in down jackets and raincoats as soon as I opened the doors at 7 a.m. They slung their backpacks onto the tables and peeled off their coats. Giggles and chatter rippled through the group as they stashed their stuff and got in line to order.

"Chai latte for me. With a cinnamon roll."

"So glad you're back, Gracie! I'll have an iced latte with oat milk and two beignets."

"Can I have the French toast sticks? Gimme a hot chocolate with that."

Beck moved easily and effortlessly, quickly processing

the orders on the espresso machine and putting them on the counter for pickup. I filled bags and containers from the display case, periodically running back to pull cinnamon rolls from the oven and French toast sticks from the cooling racks.

"Anybody missing a hazelnut latte?" I called out, raising my voice above the room's roar of conversation. I read the name Beck had scrawled on the remaining cup on the counter. "The cup says Dakota."

"That's me!" A young woman with a mop of curly black hair popped up from a table and came to get it. "Started talking and totally forgot."

Today I was happy to see the teenagers. Their energy, chatter and sense of humor were exactly what I needed.

Chloe Westerman, Police Chief Westerman's grand-daughter, came in a few minutes late today. She looked tired. I wondered if she'd stayed up late to do homework, since she'd spent her weekend working at the bakery.

"G'morning, Gracie. Welcome back."

I reached across the counter to give her a side hug. "Hey, thanks for working through the weekend. You guys did a great job of handling those crowds."

"It was a lot of fun. I couldn't believe how many people came in. Too bad Aiden slept in." She rolled her eyes. "But I learned how to make cinnamon rolls! Beck helped me with the dough. I'm going to try making them at home this week."

"Look at you. You're a baker, now" I said, giving her an air high five.

"I love it," she smiled softly. She picked up her hazelnut latte and cinnamon roll from the counter. "Beck's a good teacher. I'm learning a lot. She showed me a TikTok of this crazy guy making sourdough and told me she'd work with me on it." She looked at me, curious. "She said something about him coming in to teach a class here?"

Chloe had seemed fascinated by the baking side of things since she'd first come into The Laughing Loaf. We only had room for eight students in the class, and I'd already invited the food blogger and YouTube reviewer.

I'd stowed the flyer under the counter. I reached down and pulled one out for Chloe.

"Here you go. The class is next weekend. Daniel's great with sourdough and very entertaining. If you want to take the class, you're in."

Chloe looked blankly at my face. "Really? I can take the class? Wait, my mom's out of town, visiting friends in LA. Do I get my grandfather to sign a permission slip or something?"

"Don't worry about that. I'll talk to him." I watched a smile grow on her face as she realized she could actually attend. "I'm excited to have you in the class. It's in my best interest to have you learn more about bread, right? Get that back to me later. We've got limited space, so first come first serve."

Chloe brightened and walked away slowly with her coffee and roll, as she studied the form.

After the students gathered up their packs and left, I asked Beck to make me an espresso shot, then I went back to check on the Mediterranean scones and cinnamon rolls. I'd baked a dozen and a half of the savory scones, just to try them out. I figured the adults would be more interested in the savory treat. I slid a tray of them into the display case.

Mayor C was one of the first to notice them when she came in this morning in her bright yellow down jacket. After ordering her oat milk latte, she perused the display case with her eagle eye.

"What's that?" She frowned and pointed out the tray of new scones. "Something new?"

"Just invented it, Corrine. It's a savory scone, made with feta and dill."

"I like the sound of that. I'll take one." She watched as I pulled out a scone and put it on a plate. "How was your time off? I heard you went up to Sonoma."

"Just great." I showed what must have been a weak smile. I hadn't told her anything specific about my getaway, but news circulates fast in River Grove. I'm sure word had gotten around town that I'd gone up to Sonoma with Nate. "But I'm glad to be back."

Mayor C sniffed at the scone on the plate and glanced at me suspiciously. She seemed to be on a fact-finding mission. "I tried to contact Nate about the softball team, but his voicemail says he's out of town. Did he stay up in Sonoma?"

"He had a photo shoot in Oregon. I think he left this morning." I sighed. "He'll be up there till Friday."

"Hmm. A little strange that he'd leave again for a long trip so soon after you got back." Mayor C watched me as she took a sip of her latte.

Just when I was close to telling the mayor to mind her own damn business, Chief Westerman came in the door.

"You didn't order for me, did you?" he asked the mayor as he shouldered his way to the front.

"You didn't get back to me when I asked you what you wanted." Mayor C responded huffily. The two of them often sounded like an old married couple, though their deepest bond was an undying commitment to fighting crime in River Grove.

The chief leaned toward the counter and sighed heavily. "Gracie, I'll take a regular latte and, I guess--one of those kale tart things."

I stared back at him with what must have been a look of shock. It was hard to believe I'd heard him correctly.

"W-what did you say, Chief?"

Since The Laughing Loaf had opened, the Chief had ordered the sweetest drinks on the menu, along with at least three beignets a day.

The Chief grimaced as he slid his credit card into the pay station. "I took some tests. On Thursday, my doctor said I need to cut the sugar. It's not easy. The worst was that damn Pastry Fest. I had to stay away completely. You know how hard that was?"

"I'm sorry you had to miss it, Chief. I know how much you like the beignets."

The Chief shook his head. "This is gonna be tough. A big change."

I expected to hear back soon that the City Hall holiday party would require a very different set of treats.

"Hang in there, Chief. The kale tart is a Beck special. It's really good."

The chief gave me a skeptical look and picked up his latte, while I pulled out and plated a tart for him.

Meanwhile, the mayor had gotten impatient and headed for the duo's usual corner table. Last year, I'd told the mayor and the chief that the corner table in the dining room was probably the best spot in the bakery to discuss urgent and confidential crime matters, so it became their morning hangout. At 8:30–9 a.m., the crime fighting duo regularly came in, ordered, and staked out their spot, often opening up a map of the town and laying out any relevant photo exhibits while they strategized.

With the cold weather this morning, the line of down-jacketed townspeople grew longer. Every time the door opened, a gust of cold air whooshed in. Everyone wanted coffee and something hot and fresh.

Beck and I kept busy serving until 10:30 a.m., when we were completely out of cinnamon rolls, apple tarts and sweet scones. I pulled scone trays out of the freezer to bake. I kneaded and prepped bread for tomorrow morning's bake.

I was laying scones out on the cooling rack when Beck stood in the doorway to the back room. She had an uncertain look on her face.

"Gracie, there's someone at the counter to see you."

From the anxious look on her face, I couldn't imagine who it might be. Someone Beck didn't know—or didn't know well. Though the first names to pop into my head were the federal marshals Jeremy and Maura—or maybe even the local contact the marshals had told me about—as yet unidentified. My father and I were still debating between ourselves who in town might be this mysterious contact.

"Who's here?"

"It's Elana. Elana Schiffer." I hadn't talked about my falling out with Elana. I wondered if Beck had picked it up. Elana hadn't come around the bakery in almost two months.

I walked out to the front, my heart pounding. I hadn't seen Elana since the night back in October when she'd dropped me off at my house, angry.

She stood at the counter, in a gold-zippered black, puffy down jacket. She looked like she was on her way to work. Her lips were lined with dark red lip gloss which stood out on her pale face. She looked nervous.

"Gracie." She nodded curtly.

"Elana, good to see you."

She looked uncomfortable. When she spoke, her tone was businesslike.

"I heard Daniel Bordleman is teaching a sourdough class here next weekend. Kirk and I are big fans of Night Rose. We go there whenever we're up in Sonoma for wine. If there's still room, I'd like to take the class."

I pictured trying to rein in Daniel and his over-the-top ways at the class while navigating awkward conversation with Elana. I wanted to tell her the class was full. I'd have enough on my mind without her being there.

I paused for a moment, watching Beck cheerfully hand a latte to Rick Vega, one of our pickiest and most annoying customers. Someone who regularly returned to the counter to complain that his drink wasn't hot enough or that he'd been cheated because his beignet didn't have enough filling. Despite the trouble he regularly caused her, Beck always smiled and told him to have a great day.

With a reluctant sigh, I reached down to pull the class flyer from under the counter.

"Sure. Here's the form. Fill this out and return it. Wear clothes you don't mind getting messy. We start at noon and end at 2 p.m. on Saturday. Then we're here 11-1 p.m. on Sunday. You'll take home a jar of Daniel's starter and a loaf of sourdough."

She took the form, looked it over and nodded, her lower lip twitching just a bit. "Thank you. I'm looking forward to it."

With that, Elana slipped out the front door and into the cold outside.

Not long afterwards, I saw the face of Griff Baxter, forty-something son of Scotty Baxter, celebrated winner of the 1986 River Grove Chili Cookoff. He came up to the counter and ordered a box of cinnamon rolls for his dad.

"So I hear you're going to have a sourdough class here in a few days?" Like his dad, he had a goofy grin and a calm and pleasant demeanor that set people at ease. "Is it—full? I mean, is there any room for me?"

"Sure, we have room for you, Griff."

He nodded. "I've been getting into baking. I've tried sourdough a couple of times, but I can't get my loaves to rise very much. You think this class might help me?"

I pulled out a form for him. "I think so, Griff. We mix up dough on Saturday and bake on Sunday. Fill this out and you're in."

"That's great. Thanks, Gracie. See you this weekend."

We had one spot left now. And considering the people who'd be in the room on Saturday, easygoing Griff was the best possible addition.

Chapter Ten

My online meeting with Daniel was at 2 p.m.

During lunchtime, I found myself, like Nate, wanting to think things through, out in the great outdoors.

Since there was a break in customers, Beck took over for me, and I went into Biga's pen and waited for him to calm down.

He ran circles around the pen, returning to me and licking my hand.

Is this for real? A walk? OMG! It's been days!

I finally clipped his leash onto his harness, which caused more of a flurry of activity. Biga pulled me to the side of the pen, nudging the gate panel. I think he was afraid if we didn't go right away, I'd change my mind.

We went out the back door and headed down the alley to get to the river trail. Biga knew the way very well, so he pulled me behind him as he raced ahead, occasionally stopping to sniff and water the foliage along the way. It was a cold, windy day, so we had the trail to ourselves.

I breathed in the cool, fresh air, rich with smells of

damp bark and dirt. Recent rains had contributed to the river, which rushed over the rocks and lapped higher at the riverbank. I thought about suggesting that Daniel Bordleman film some video footage of the trail. It was beautiful, and the redwoods at dusk could give him that spooky feel as well as showing a different landscape than he'd get in Sonoma.

As I passed below the back of The Riverside Saloon, its 70-plus-year-old owner, Reggie McFerrin, waved down at me as he leaned on the railing of his office balcony. He wore the standard look he wore yearlong: sunglasses, an improbably black ponytail, black jacket, and black jeans. Today, it finally seemed appropriate to the weather.

Back in October, Reggie had helped Elana and I escape from the Russian spies who came after me at The Riverside. When I first met him, I'd been skeptical of Reggie; he seemed almost sinister and looked like a hippie turned vampire—yet the people of River Grove loved him. After his quick action at The Riverside that night, I owed him my life.

We turned around before we got to the redwood grove. I had to tend to bread dough before my meeting with Daniel. I wanted to make sure he had things the way he wanted for the class. Everything I knew about him and Night Rose told me he'd be hard to work with if he didn't have the right resources and setup for teaching. I'd make sure to go over everything in our call.

When I returned to The Laughing Loaf, I felt refreshed and settled. I put Biga back in his pen and made him jump and then sit for some liver treats. Then I washed my hands and got to work on the bread dough. After proofing, my brioche loaves were now ready to bake, so I slid them on trays into the oven, looking forward to savoring the rich, buttery smell of the bake. That smell literally lured customers in from off the street.

A little before 2 p.m., as Beck worked on her tart shells, I went into my tiny office off the back room and prepared for the Zoom. Daniel entered the online waiting room, and I clicked to let him in. The stark lighting in his office made him look shadowed and eerie, like he was in one of his YouTube videos.

"Gracie, I'm short on time today." He looked at someone off to his left. "Unfortunately, I have someone I have to meet with today. I want to pin down as much as possible for Saturday."

"Me, too," I said, pausing to hit record for our Zoom meeting. I wanted to make sure I had all Daniel's demands on the record.

This would be a stretch for us. There was no way we could do the class while the bakery was open, so we'd close Saturday at 10:30 a.m. Then Beck and I would join the class. Eight students would line up along two tables, each with a bag of flour and a plastic Cambro tub for mixing the dough. I told him the flour brand, which was my usual, and the gluten content in the flour to make sure it met his standards. He raised his eyebrows.

"I wished you'd asked me before you ordered," he said bluntly, frowning. "Though I suppose the quality's adequate for what we're doing. Tell me about our students."

I told him about the food blogger and the YouTuber.

"Excellent call," he said, steepling his fingers like an arch villain. "The more publicity the better. I know them both. We should get some mileage out of this."

I told him about Beck, Chloe, and then the addition of Elana, one of Night Rose's biggest fans. Then, when we were busy yesterday, I'd gotten a call from a man who said he'd attended the woodfired class with me at Night Rose and would be in the area. That would take our last spot.

"A man from the woodfired oven class saw this on the Night Rose website and asked if he could attend."

Daniel flinched, then he scowled at someone or something to his left. He sighed. "Whatever. We've got a full class then. Omar will help work with the students."

Unlike Rafal, Omar was apparently still in Daniel's good graces. I wondered about Ashley, the woman who'd stormed out of the front door of Night Rose the morning of the class.

I wanted to be able to tell Beck what time to be here, so I asked about the video.

"You're filming the video when you come into town on Friday afternoon, right?" That's what he said when we'd talked back in Sonoma.

Daniel looked down at a planner on his desk.

"Now why would you think that, Gracie? I've got an appointment to fit in that day before the bookstore. No, we'll need to do the video early on Saturday—8 a.m. I'll have Ashley get some footage outside and around town, but I need to have a baking setup inside and full use of the oven."

What the heck? That was going to be tough at that hour. The bakery would be open, and Saturday mornings were the busiest time of the week.

"We can't do it then, Daniel. We'll be open for business. We'll need to use our oven. You're coming into town on Friday night. I remember you saying we could do it then."

I thought smoke was going to pour out of Daniel Bordleman's mouth and ears. He glared at me.

"Gracie, let me remind you that you proposed this class to me. And I agreed to do it on short notice. Do you want to make this work or not? Do you have any idea how much this will benefit your little business? What my name and Night Rose's reputation will do for you? This is going to take your tiny bakery in the sticks and put it on the map." He leaned toward the screen, his eyes narrowed. "You should be grateful. Now do you want that or not?" He settled back into his seat, his arms crossed expectantly.

What could I say? At this point, I'd committed to this. I'd planned to close the bakery and invited the blogger and YouTube reviewer. Excited students were planning on attending. This was a big deal—Daniel was a celebrity baker and the whole town was excited about his appearance at The Laughing Loaf. I couldn't back out now.

"Okay, Daniel. We'll work it out. You'll have access to the oven and a place to film in the baking area from 8 a.m. till the class." I wasn't quite sure yet how that would work. It would require some late hours the night before—or a very early morning for Beck and me.

"I'm glad you've come around on this," he said, with an arrogant tilt of his chin "This is a big opportunity for you, Gracie. Don't blow it."

I heard somebody mumbling something off the screen. Night Rose was a busy bakery, and Daniel was probably being summoned.

After ending the call, I leaned back in my chair, brushed my hair off my face and groaned.

Beck came over from where she'd been making the apple tarts, pulled over a stool, and plunked down. Her dark eyes were wide with shock.

"Gracie, I heard everything." She frowned and shook her head. "Daniel sounded so full of himself. Is that what he's really like? Now I'm sorry that I recommended him to you."

I sat up and smiled wryly at her. "Don't be sorry, Beck. He's right. I did invite him to come here, and he accommodated us on very short notice. I still think we can learn a lot from him. He's a great baker. After you get the tarts prepped, let's figure out how we can make this work and keep the bakery open."

After some discussion, we decided to come back Friday evening to get as much baked as we could in advance. It meant some things wouldn't be as fresh as usual for Saturday morning, but we'd isolate what absolutely had to be done that morning—like beignets and cinnamon rolls—and work with that.

Beck went back to her table to roll out beignet dough. "This will be an adventure."

I snorted. "That's one way to look at it. I just hope it's worth the trouble."

"I can't believe Daniel said he would put The Laughing Loaf on the map," Beck said indignantly. "We're already on the map!"

She was right, locally anyway. Thanks to some mentions in area newspapers, we were now getting a regular flow of out of towners.

We weren't Night Rose. Maybe we'd never be. But if being like Daniel Bordleman was the price of that success, I didn't want it.

THAT NIGHT, I hoped I'd hear something from Nate.

A creature of habit, Nate often called or texted at 9 p.m., which for him, for some reason, was Gracie time. To keep my mind off it, I sat down at my desk and pulled up my business accounting system on my laptop, to track the month's revenue. This cheered me up; we'd gotten a nice bump from Winter Pastry Fest. Then I flopped down on the bed and cuddled with Biga while I read up on the science of sourdough, something about Daniel's videos I found intriguing.

At 9:05, my phone lit up with a text. My heart leaped. I grabbed the phone quickly, only to find it was a confirmation for an upcoming dentist appointment in Santa Cruz.

I buried my head in my pillow. Biga moved closer to me, mostly just for warmth.

It was going to be a long week.

Chapter Eleven

Friday, December 13

The week sped by, as I ordered ingredients and gathered all the Cambro tubs I could find for the students to mix dough in.

Beck and I strategized the layout of the back room for the class and sketched out a diagram so we could set up as soon as we finished our bakes for Saturday.

Around noon that Friday, I got a call from Ashley Fontaine, who wanted to come over to check out the baking space for the video. She and Daniel were checking in to their rental in River Grove at 3 p.m., so she'd come over afterwards. She'd bring Daniel's props and a costume and wig for Beck.

Beck had gone home for a break before returning for our Friday night bake-a-thon. I was prepping for the bakes when Ashley knocked on the back door of the bakery. I opened the door to a woman with long blonde hair, a little taller than me and in her mid-twenties—definitely the woman I saw stomping out of Night Rose. She wore a trench coat with a large video camera bag strapped across her chest and was grunting as she struggled to heave an overstuffed carry-on bag up the steps.

"Ashley? I'm Gracie Markley, owner of The Laughing Loaf. Let me help you with that." I helped her lift the bag up over the last step into the back room.

"River Grove is sure a cute little town," she said, as she unbuttoned her coat. "After this, I'll go out and shoot some background footage for the video. Daniel's going to be focused on the teaching, so he's left the other parts to me."

I was curious about Ashley Fontaine, from what I'd heard from Maeve. Add to that, the fact that anyone who could stay married to Daniel had to be an interesting person. Or just crazy.

"What's your background, Ashley? Did you start out in film?"

"Oh, God, no," she laughed heartily. "My background's in business, and I was doing makeup and hair for community theatre when I met Daniel. He told me he wanted to start doing YouTube videos and that I was going to film him. So I learned how to do it really quick."

"Wait. Aren't you assistant manager of Night Rose?" As Laughing Loaf's assistant manager, Beck was an important part of the baking team.

"I am, but I mostly manage employees. You would not believe how hard that is. I mean, you give them an inch and they just walk all over you. We've had such a hard time hiring and keeping good people."

I looked at her skeptically. "When I visited, I was impressed by Night Rose's staff. Maeve, Rafal, and Omar. Everyone seemed friendly and very competent."

Ashley frowned at me. "How can you possibly know what we deal with at the bakery every day? Rafal lied to us, on a regular basis—so Daniel had to fire him. Maeve whines constantly. They should be grateful for the opportunity to work at a bakery with our reputation."

She pulled the carry-on into the back room and hefted it up onto a side table. When she unzipped it, I saw thick, folded black cloth, a skeleton hand, and clear plastic packets of what looked like fake blood. She pulled out a very tall, fluffy wig in a box, then a shiny black dress with purple trim.

"This is for your assistant, Becky," she said, passing it to me.

"Beck," I corrected her. "Her name is Beck."

She sighed heavily as she dug through the case. "Yeah, that's what I said. *Becky*. Make sure she gets the costume and is here ready to roll at 7 a.m. I'll need to do her makeup."

She stacked the backdrop on the table, along with an oversized skull, the skeleton hand, and a handful of fuzzy tarantulas. Not real, thankfully. She pulled out her phone and scrolled through a message.

"I'm going to check out the town and get some footage while it's light. Then I'm meeting up with Daniel at the rental house. Any decent restaurants around this town?"

"I'd try the Riverside Saloon, right across the street," I said, but she looked like she hadn't waited for my reply. She was scrolling on her phone. "They're open late. They have really good comfort food and drinks."

"Huh. I see a pizza place here—some place called RGs?"

I snickered mentally. If she wasn't going to listen to me, then she deserved an overcooked pizza with artificial cheese topping at RGs.

"I know you don't have much time, Ashley. Need any suggestions on what to film locally?" I asked. "There are some great spots down by the river—along the river trail. You can get some spooky shots in the redwoods."

"I don't need your suggestions. I know exactly what Daniel wants." She looked at me directly. "I'll be back with Daniel at 7 a.m., so have everything set up for tomorrow morning."

With that, Ashley Fontaine buttoned up her coat and hurried out the back door.

I'd see if Chloe Westerman and Aiden could come in early to work the register and espresso machine the next morning, since Beck would be working on the video with Daniel, and I'd be helping to set up for class.

I wondered what I'd gotten myself into.

And if anything good could come out of this weekend.

Beck came back to the bakery at 6. I'd gone across the street to pick up food at The Riverside for us: Chips and a giant bowl of Reggie's own homemade guacamole, spicy grilled chicken and macaroni and cheese with bacon bits. We'd probably be here till 11 p.m., so we needed to be fortified.

"Gracie! This smells delicious," she said as she began opening the containers of food. She picked up a paper plate and began loading up on chicken and macaroni. "You didn't have to do this."

"I appreciate you coming back to bake. And for agreeing to help tomorrow." I opened up the guacamole and scooped a very large dollop out onto my plate. I hadn't eaten much today, so it looked amazing. This would be my appetizer course. "And this is not long after Winter Pastry Fest. I know your husband would probably like to see you more often."

Beck put her hand over her mouth as she laughed with a mouth full of macaroni. She took a moment to chew and swallow. "Sam's fine with me working more hours. He's happy that I'm doing something I love. And a lot of times I make stuff for him that I make here. He's super happy to be my tester."

After we finished, I boxed up the leftovers and put them in the small aqua fridge. We washed up and I showed Beck the costume Ashley had dropped off for her.

While the oven preheated for baking scones, Beck tried on the black and purple dress. Her thin brown arms peered out from the long, heavy sleeves, and once I helped her secure the ties at the back, the dress fit her well. For a creepy dress, it actually looked beautiful on her slim frame. Silver bands woven through the fabric caught the light and made it look like she was electrified.

"Want to try the wig?"

Beck doubtfully eyed the black and purple wig of hair piled a foot and a half high. "How is this supposed to stay on my head?"

"Looks like you're supposed to be the Bride of Frankenstein," I said, looking on the inside of the wig to see what would secure it. There were several clips. "Let's try it. Maybe Ashley can help tomorrow. By the way, she wants to do your makeup, too."

"Oh my God, Gracie," she moaned. "Why did I agree to do this?" Her moaning didn't take away from the excited look on her young face. She was so looking forward to this.

I pulled my office chair away from my desk. "Let's try it. Sit down. That'll make it easier for me to reach your head."

Beck gingerly sat down on my office chair. I twirled her ponytail into a spiral and pinned it down on her head with bobby pins. Then I set the very high wig gently on her head and slid the clips in against her scalp to secure it. Beck looked afraid to move. She turned her eyes up to me.

"Is it on? Can I move now?"

I clasped my hands together. "Beck, this looks great on you!"

She frowned up at me without moving her head a centimeter. "Seriously? I feel like it's going to look weird."

"Now stay. Don't move." I ran into the women's restroom, where I kept a hand mirror in a drawer. I brought it back and handed it to her. She held it up.

"Wow." She said softly turning her head a bit to look at herself. "This looks so strange, but—I kind of like it."

I pulled out my phone, backed away a few steps, and took her photo.

"This is the whole look." I showed her the photo. Her sitting with the gorgeous dress on, sparkling under the lights, her hair shooting up to the sky in a precarious dramatic, sparkling beehive. Sweet, cheerful Beck was now a goth queen. Needless to say, it was a new look for Beck. She looked amazing.

Beck was speechless for a moment. "I look pretty. And also scary."

"Well, you are pretty." I laughed. "And sometimes a little scary, too. Especially when you're flipping those beignets in the hot oil in the morning. Want me to send this to Sam?"

Beck's face turned pink. "No!" Then she reconsidered, a faint smile on her face. "Okay. Yes. Send it to him."

I pulled up Sam's contact on my phone and hit send, giggling like one of the teenagers at Laughing Loaf early weekday mornings.

"You should probably hang the costume up to get the wrinkles out. Then let's get to work."

While singing along to a soundtrack of 1980s pop, we worked on everything we need to bake tonight and have ready for the oven in the morning. Beck assembled apple tarts and frittata cups and prepped the fillings. I baked scones and the loaves of brioche and country bread until I'd filled all our cooling racks. The music energized us, and we chatted as we worked.

Beck gave me the scoop on what it was like growing up with older brothers—constant teasing, a few pranks along with some sweet moments. She also told me when she'd met Sam, her parents hadn't approved of him. They'd begun to change their opinion of him when he told them he wanted to refinish her family's dining table and put it in the house he planned to buy for him and Beck when they got married. Then he showed them his bank statement: he had the cash to buy it.

At 11:15 p.m., we finished up the last trays of the apple tarts. If Nate had texted at 9, I wouldn't know since I hadn't checked my phone since I sent Beck's photo.

We were both exhausted but feeling much better about tomorrow's class. I'd been up since 4:30 a.m. I was punchy and bone tired. But we'd done everything we'd needed to do. Daniel could have the back room, for the most part, and the oven.

"I'm scared about tomorrow," Beck said, stifling a yawn. "I don't like Daniel anymore."

"I get that." I nodded as I wiped down the metal table. "I want to learn all I can from him. After Sunday, I'll be happy if I never see Daniel Bordleman again." I went back to the fridge for one last dip of Reggie's guacamole—the direct method this time, no chip required, just a spoon.

It turned out I'd get my wish.

Chapter Twelve

Saturday, December 14

Chief Westerman's truck rumbled over the gravel in the alley at 6:45 a.m. that morning, pulling to a stop with a crunch.

I poked my head out the door and waved at the police chief as Chloe jumped out, blonde braids flying. She slammed the door and made her way up the steps. Her breath formed clouds in the cold, early morning air.

I gratefully ushered her up front to start getting ready for opening. She wasn't as fast as Beck on the espresso machine, but she was detail-oriented and a fast learner.

Beck and I had come in at 5 a.m., so neither of us had had a full night's sleep. We kept the music pumping and pushed through our duties with nervous energy. I filled the display case with trays of just-baked cinnamon rolls and the beignets Beck had just fried up. The pumpkin filled ones, still in demand, filled the bakery with a rich, creamy spicy scent.

A few people in down jackets stood outside around the outside tables at the front of the bakery talking, waiting for the us to open. Every time I glanced outside, more people were milling around, waiting. As I suspected, it would be a busy Saturday morning. We'd be working hard right up until Daniel's class.

I put out the Laughing Loaf Joke of the Day. It was a joke Elana would laugh at, which made me a little sad. Maybe we'd both be so focused on the lesson, we wouldn't have time to talk to each other. I hoped that, anyway, since I had absolutely no idea what I'd say to her.

Laughing Loaf Joke of the Day
Last night I accidentally drank a bottle of invisible ink.
Now I'm in the hospital waiting to be seen.

"Gracie, good morning." Mayor C was first in line at the counter and appearing unusually jovial. Her cheeks were rosy from the cold outside. "The usual for me. Today's the big day, huh?"

I called the mayor's hazelnut latte order over to Chloe, who gave me a thumbs up.

"Yep. Daniel and his assistant will be here any minute. They'll start filming one of his YouTube videos here first. Beck's playing Bride of Frankenstein."

The mayor tried to look past me to see what was going on in the back room.

She chuckled. "I can't imagine that. I'll look forward to the video. Hope it goes well today."

"Meeting with the Chief today?" I pulled a kale frittata out with tongs and slid it onto a plate.

"Dave thinks of The Laughing Loaf as more of a temptation now than a place to meet," the mayor said with a sigh. "The doctors told him he has to make some big changes to his diet. He tried the kale frittata and hated it."

I frowned. Great. I couldn't think of anything else he could eat here. I'd fry him up an egg from one of Beck's chickens if that would keep him coming back for his and the mayor's crime and safety meetings.

Mayor C took her drink and frittata and searched for a table. A couple had nabbed the corner table. Mayor C stood nearby and tapped her foot, as she scrolled through messages on her phone. The couple looked up at the mayor then exchanged nervous glances. They stood up suddenly and looked for another spot.

At 7:15, I told Chloe to handle orders, then I went back to see how things were going in the back room.

Painfully bright photography lights had been set up on stands around the back table. A tall metal frame held up a black backdrop behind the table. Beck sat nearby in my office chair, wearing the black and purple dress, and a plastic cape over her shoulders which was secured up around her neck. Her hair was pulled up into a ponytail. Ashley was applying a thick coat of white makeup to Beck's face.

Beck looked pale and ghostly, her brown eyes looking unnaturally large and dark in her new white face as she tried to hold perfectly still.

"I'm starting to get nervous," Beck said, as Ashley daubed the makeup around her hairline with expert little strokes. "I've never acted in anything before. What if I make a mistake and mess the whole thing up?"

Ashley smiled as she began applying dark purple eyeshadow to Beck's eyelids. "Just relax and read the lines Omar's going to hold up on the cards. You're going to look great. Daniel can be a little demanding. Don't pay any attention to him." The woman touched Beck's hand reassuringly. "You've got this, hon."

When I saw Beck fully made up, her wig rising up off her head in a dramatic, sparkling tower, I wondered why Ashley Fontaine was working as an assistant manager at a bakery and not as a makeup artist for a theatre company.

"You doing okay, Beck?" I bent down next to the chair and asked my assistant.

"I'm fine, Gracie," she responded softly, trying not to move her head. "Ashley made me feel better. I think I can do this."

Daniel Bordleman had donned a Frankenstein outfit – a too-small black suit with a ripped ruffled shirt exposing a chest painted green with makeup.

"Will you please give us some space here, Gracie?" Daniel said impatiently, holding a sheaf of notes. "We'll be baking the final bread we'll show in the video in about a half hour, so the less traffic in here the better."

My cheeks burned. This was my bakery. And, yes, I know I did invite this guy here, and now I was regretting it.

I looked at the big clock over the fridge. 8 a.m.. Two hours till we could close and then focus on the class. My takeaway, which I hoped would make this all worth it, would be learning new techniques from Daniel.

I went back out to the front counter, where Chloe shot me an anxious look. There was a line stretching out beyond the door. A light rain had started, so customers outside were huddled under the awning to keep dry. Customers inside at the tables were staying put, drinking their coffee and looking out at their fellow townspeople; they were inside and dry, and they knew they had a good thing.

As I pulled out pastries and bread loaves for customers, Daniel's theatrical baritone voice bellowed from the back room.

"Dear God! What has made this creature come to life?"

Then Beck, after what sounded like some coaching:

"It has grown! Heat and the yeast of the air has made it so, my lord!"

Then Daniel continued, clapping his hands and explaining the process of the two elements in the dough—the wild yeast in the starter and the bacteria that helped produce the sugar. How the yeast caused the web of gluten strands to rise.

Customers could hear their voices, too. Some people in line looked puzzled, some laughed.

"A baker from up north is filming a YouTube video in the back," I explained, with a smile. "Beck is back there, dressed as Bride of Frankenstein."

Jack and Jeanne Daniels of Speed Spot Motors were in line, waiting to order. "Now that's something I'd like to see," Jeanne said with a giggle.

Soon, Ashley came out to the front, indignant. "You need to be quiet. We're picking up noise from the front on our recording. Keep the door closed. We're ready to do a final recording."

I groaned under my breath.

A half hour later, Ashley came out and announced that they were done and had all the footage they needed. It was 9:30. "We need to get everything put away for the class setup. We'll need your help to clean up."

"You'll have to wait a half hour, Ashley," I said. "We're packed today. I can't help you till we close."

Ashley gave me a stare of exasperation. She stomped to the back room.

After closing, I hung a sign on the front door: CLOSED FOR PRIVATE EVENT, but kept it unlocked for the sourdough class students arriving. I breathed a sigh of relief.

I went to the back room and saw that Omar from Night

Rose had arrived and was working with Ashley to tear down the backdrop, lights, and sound equipment. The room was starting to look like my baking room again.

They left the tripod with the video camera up, to film the class.

Beck was still dressed as the bride, wig and all. She had a big smile on her very white face as she talked to Omar, who by the looks of it, was flirting with her. She lifted her skirt daintily as she made her way over to me.

She lowered her voice, but her eyes gleamed with excitement. "Okay, that was so much fun. I can't believe how many times we had to do it before we got it right, though. I'm ready to give up acting and go back to baking."

She retrieved her clothes and apron from my office and headed for the women's restroom to change.

Daniel came out of the men's restroom wearing a tidy white chef's coat, apron and jeans. The green monster makeup was gone, and his face looked freshly scrubbed and pink. He stood over by Ashley. She glanced up at him with an expectant look, maybe looking for some thanks for all her work—but he picked up his phone with a frown and started twirling his thumbs over it. It looked like he was texting someone. He did not look happy.

"The footage we got should be adequate," Daniel looked up from the phone when I approached him. "Unfortunately, we had to do several takes with your assistant, but I think we got something we can work with. Now we'll need help setting up the tables for the students."

Chloe came back to help and together we got a station set up for each student, complete with a flour tub, jar of Daniel's starter, and a round, see-through Cambro tub for mixing dough. I looked around at the room with satisfaction. Okay, we'd survived the video filming. The room looked tidy and there was space for each student to work.

I brought back baked goods from the display case to snack on, and Chloe took orders for espresso drinks. Beck, back to her normal clothes and skin color, brought out a pitcher of ice water and helped lay out a tray with ham, turkey, cheese and tomato slices for people to make sandwiches. I sliced some Laughing Loaf brioche and sourdough loaves and brought out paper plates and condiments. Ashley, Omar, and Daniel began piling their plates with food.

Students started arriving at 11:45. The first was Susan Federer, the food blogger. The 50-something woman with a grey Dutch Boy haircut looked starstruck to meet Daniel in person. She gushed as she talked about her visits to Night Rose and the flavors of the bakery's sourdough.

Daniel ate it up. In that weird way I'd seen him do at Night Rose, he morphed from a jerk to a really friendly guy.

"Why, Susan, thank you for your kind words," he oozed in an unctuous voice, grasping her hand with both of his. "I'm thrilled to finally meet you in person."

Koa Wilson from Eureka showed up next, after knocking on the back door. I let him in and greeted him warmly. As he had that day at Night Rose, he wore a red bandana wrapped around his head and a denim apron over a long linen tunic. He had the fresh smell of laundry that had dried outside in the sun.

"Thanks for coming all this way, Koa," I said, after I gave him a hug. "How long was your drive?"

He waved his hand dismissively. "About six and a half hours. A college friend and I switched off with the driving, since he was coming down to visit friends in Santa Cruz."

Griff Baxter and Elana came into the room from the

front entrance next. It looked like they'd driven over together, which made sense, since the Baxters were just a few blocks down the street from the Schiffers. They were chatting and smiling, which I took as a good sign.

But as soon as Elana's eyes connected with mine, her face froze. She set her purse down on the stool next to Griff Baxter and rushed to the front to greet Daniel, with the same smitten look Susan had.

Griff, on the other hand, remained on his stool, legs swinging, smiling at everyone as he looked around the room expectantly. Between the tension radiating from Daniel, Ashley and Elana, I was relieved that Griff was here.

The only one who wasn't here yet was the YouTuber, Marco Bardugo. He was driving down from Oakland, so he might have hit some of the bad weekend traffic on Highway 880. Marco did video reviews of restaurants and bakeries. He'd done a few reviews on Night Rose. I'd happened to meet him when he came to River Grove during the summer, to include The Laughing Loaf in a review of off-the-beaten-path bakeries.

As Daniel waited to start the demonstration, Ashley set the video camera on its tripod to record the class. She used it to pan across the room, recording footage of the students.

From behind his demonstration table, Daniel waved me over. He had the same setup as everyone else—a jar of sourdough starter, a plastic Cambro tub and flour.

"The YouTuber, Marco, isn't here. You told me you invited him. Where is he?" Daniel hissed.

"We're still waiting for him," I said, checking my phone for any text he might have sent. "If he's not here in ten minutes, you should start. I don't want to hold up the rest of the group."

"We need to wait," Daniel said with a note of arrogance

in his voice. "I want Marco here. He's handling the publicity for this. Let me call him." He pulled out his phone and clicked on a contact.

"Marco, where are you, bud?" After a pause, Daniel laughed as if Marco had just shot back a hilarious response. "Gotcha, see you soon."

"Five minutes." He looked at me triumphantly.

"Let me do an intro," I told him in a low voice before he had a chance to stop me. "Then we'll go around the room and get everyone's name."

I stepped out in front of Daniel's demonstration table.

"Glad to see everyone here," I began, looking out at the eager students at the two long tables. "This is our first ever baking class, and I'm happy to welcome Daniel Bordleman, owner of Night Rose in Sonoma County, which specializes in artisanal sourdough breads. Daniel's got his own YouTube channel, and before class, we filmed a video here at the Laughing Loaf. He's just released his first baking book, *Night of the Living Bread*. Welcome, Daniel Bordleman. Thank you for being here."

The students erupted in enthusiastic applause, and Daniel received it all with a smug look on his face. It was a pretty gracious introduction, if I can pat myself on the back.

The students introduced themselves then talked about their baking experience, which apart from me, Beck, and Susan, wasn't much.

"What you learn today, you will be able to use right away. I'll teach you a foolproof way to make your own starter. After learning these techniques, you'll be making your own sourdough within a few weeks. You won't need to buy yeast since your starter will be collecting wild yeast from the air. And of course, after you start making bread, grocery store bread won't even taste like bread to you anymore."

The class laughed.

Before even worrying about mixing bread dough, Daniel showed the group how to mix the starter by holding up a jar and adding equal parts of flour and water. He stirred the mixture and covered it loosely.

"See? Easy. You'll need to set it in a warm place and discard half of it after two days—then add the equal parts of flour and water with the remaining starter. You're feeding the yeast, which needs to eat. Just like all of us." Scattered light laughter from the students. Daniel held up the fed starter that everyone had at their station, which had bubbles in it. "Finally, it'll look like this." Then he took a spoonful of starter and dropped it into a clear glass of water. He held it up so we could all see the blob floating.

"See? When the starter is ready to bake with, a spoonful of it will float in the water."

We started with the fed starter in the jar in front of us, and followed his instructions for mixing the dough, by mixing flour with warm water—which Omar and Ashley brought by in insulated pitchers.

"While we wait a half hour for the dough to autolyze, let's talk about the science." My heart beat a little faster. This was the part I was excited about.

Daniel explained what was happening to the sticky mixture in front of us. "We don't add the starter or the salt yet. Here's what's happening in that tub in front of you before we add it—something you can't see. This is the autolyze phase, a time of rest for our dough. Enzymes are breaking down the protein in the flour to produce sugar. That sugar is absolutely irresistible to yeast. So once the starter goes in, you're going to have happy yeast, which will result in better rise and flavor. By simply letting the dough rest, you'll be ensuring a lighter, more flavorful loaf."

As we waited, a man in his 30s slunk into the back room, wearing sunglasses. He had disheveled hair and his buttoned-down shirt not tucked in. He looked like he'd woken up with a hangover. A messenger bag was slung over his shoulder. Marco Bardugo, from what I remembered from his videos. I met him at the door of the back room and steered him to the last station at the back table.

As Daniel went on the describe what would happen to the gluten strands, I noticed something odd. The bakery owner's face had looked pink after he'd come out of the bathroom, after scrubbing the makeup off his face. Now his face seemed to be turning an even deeper shade of pink.

I whispered to Beck, who was at the station next to me.

"Is it just my imagination? Does Daniel's skin look really—rosy?"

Beck nodded and whispered back. "A little. Like he's embarrassed or something."

I found this interesting, since I was sure there were few things that embarrassed Daniel.

"I'd say he's been out in the sun too long," I noted as I watched him. "But it's been raining all day."

Daniel paused for a moment in his explanation. He clutched the edge of the table for a moment for support as if he was dizzy. He nodded to Ashley, who set down the video camera and brought him a cup of water. Daniel gulped it down and continued.

We finished adding the starter and Daniel showed us how to do folds in the dough, which I was very familiar with.

"What you'll want to do now is fold the dough over on itself—stretching it. Do this in both directions. You're stretching the gluten strands, so they'll have elasticity and more room to rise. They know what to do—they will start to line up, to create a structure for the dough. Now we're going to let it rest for another half hour, so right before we leave for the day, we can give it one more stretch. Then these will rise at your stations until tomorrow morning. We'll keep the kitchen at a nice warm temperature all night—around 78 degrees."

There wasn't anything earth shattering about Daniel's teaching, other than that it helped to know the science behind what the dough was doing on its way to becoming bread.

We finished up with one last fold and stretch to our dough, then everyone put their lids on their Cambros and left them at their station for their overnight rise.

I brought out a tray of chocolate chip sourdough starter cookies I'd made this morning. I thought it would be appropriate for Daniel's talk, since the recipe included starter discard. Students crowded around the platter, talking and tasting the rich, soft cookies.

"Just something else to make with the discard from your starter," I said. "If you're going to make sourdough often, you'll end up with lots of discard. Don't let it go to waste. There are some great recipes that use it."

Daniel sat down for a while, drinking from an RG's Pizza cup, as Ashley took his mixing tub and utensils to the sink and began washing. His phone rang, and he stood up unsteadily, bracing himself against the wall, as he moved to the corner near the door to answer it.

"I can't wait to see how my loaf rises," Griff said excitedly. "Crossing my fingers. This could be the one time my bread actually turns out."

Elana spoke up, though she seemed to have a hard time

connecting with my eyes. "I hear you, Griff. I tried to make a loaf for thanksgiving dinner. It took so long to rise, I finally just put it in the oven and baked it. It came out so tough and dry."

I glanced over at Daniel, who was still talking on his phone, frowning, as he almost slumped against the wall. Koa from Eureka approached him, and Daniel gave him a look of what I can only describe as disgust. It made Koa angry, and he flounced off.

Marco Bardugo came up to him, but Daniel shook his head and gave him a twisted smile. A look of fear crossed the reviewer's face.

When Omar came over to the platter, I let him gather up a few cookies then pulled him to the side.

"Hey, Omar, is Daniel okay? He's not looking well today."

Omar looked over at his boss and gave a noncommittal shrug that seemed lacking in sympathy. "He's always working. He's always up in everyone's business—never trusts us to do our jobs. That's gotta tire a person out."

"But his skin's a weird color."

Omar took a bite of his cookie and turned around to look. "I guess? I thought it was because he'd scrubbed the makeup off from the video shoot."

Was it just my imagination? I glanced over at Beck, whose skin had also been covered in makeup for the video. She looked normal.

"You also turned up the heat so the dough can rise. It's hot in here," Omar pointed out. "Hey, these starter cookies are great, Gracie. Can I get the recipe?"

"Sure, no problem." Omar jotted down his email and handed it to me.

In a few minutes, Ashley raised her voice and addressed the group.

"People, Daniel needs to leave now. He has his signing at the bookstore in Santa Cruz. We'll see you all tomorrow morning at 11 a.m.—not noon, remember. Your dough will be ready, and we'll start the baking process."

The students murmured amongst themselves, and most of them grabbed a couple of cookies and a napkin for the road, then made their way to the front door of the bakery. Susan Federer called out, "Thank you, Daniel," which prompted a chorus of thanks from the small group.

Griff came over to me, like a big friendly dog, while Elana waited by the door of the back room. "Thanks for letting me into the class, Gracie. I'm real excited about tomorrow's bake."

Daniel put his phone away. Ashley was stuffing the props and backdrops into the rolling suitcase. She zipped it up, then pulled up the handle. She set it down on the floor and began tugging it behind her.

I walked out of the back room with Daniel, Ashley and Omar, as they headed to the front.

"We'll see you tomorrow. Hope you get some good sleep tonight, Daniel. Can I get you any water for the road?"

"We're fine, Gracie." Ashley said impatiently as she steered Daniel toward the front. He looked unstable on his feet. "We have water."

* * *

FIVE MINUTES LATER, Beck, Chloe and I were cleaning up the front for tomorrow's opening.

"So glad that's over," I'd just taken a mop to the dining room floor to wipe up a coffee spill.

I looked up as I heard pounding on the front door. Through the front door window, I saw Ashley's horrified face. I ran to open it.

Ashley was breathing in and out fast, like she was hyperventilating.

"D-Daniel's in the car. He'd just sat down. Next thing I saw, he slumped over in his seat." She wiped at a trail of mascara running down her face. "I just called 911. I picked up his wrist and couldn't feel any pulse."

I ran out the door to see Chief Westerman pull up at the curb in the RGPD squad car. EMTs from the county wheeled up in a van right behind the Chief.

I ran outside and stood under the awning, trying to stay out of the way of the responders.

EMTs darted toward the passenger side of the car. They were talking to Ashley, who had crumpled down to the curb in front of Daniel with a guttural wail. They were trying to convince her to move out of the way, so they could get to the baker.

It was like a scene from of an over-the-top movie. After Ashley Fontaine's dramatic collapse, one of the EMTs went around and opened the driver's door to reach Daniel.

Finally, the Chief gently helped Ashley up. With his hands on her back and arm, he guided her to the sidewalk, so the EMTs could attend to Daniel.

"Oh my God! Daniel!" Ashley tried to wrest herself away from the Chief.

"Ashley, this isn't helping Daniel." Omar spoke to her softly. He put his hand on her arm and she flung it off.

"Ma'am, the EMTs need to do their job," the Chief was saying, then she finally stopped fighting him. "You say this is your husband?"

"Yes. His name is Daniel Bordleman. I'm his wife, Ashley Fontaine."

"The medical examiner will be here in a few minutes, Ashley," the Chief said, in a calming voice. "I'll stay right here with you. Can you tell me what happened right before this? Had he been sick? Any breathing issues?"

"No, nothing." Ashley's mascara had smeared down her face. "He'd just finished teaching a class at the bakery here."

"A couple of us noticed his skin was very pink during the talk," I said. As if on cue, Beck and Chloe came out of the bakery and stood nearby.

The Chief looked at me, then shot a look at Daniel's body. "He is pink. Bright pink."

One of the EMTs stepped back. He frowned as if trying to remember something. "Was your husband around a lot of smoke in the past 24 hours—from a house or wildfire?"

It seemed like a random question. Ashley shook her head and continued heaving. "No. Not at all."

The EMT continued. "It's the skin color. I've seen a case of it, a man we rescued from a house fire. His body wasn't processing oxygen. The oxygen stayed in the blood, but it was never transferred to the cells. That's what causes the bright pink color."

"What would cause it to not process the oxygen?" I asked.

The EMT looked over at the Chief, grimly.

"Cyanide."

Chapter Thirteen

The county medical examiner arrived and took a look at the celebrity baker's body, now on a stretcher in the ambulance. The examiner was tight-lipped when he came out of the vehicle. The Chief took him aside and they spoke in low tones. EMTs shut the doors and started the ambulance up with a rumble, ready to take Daniel's body away.

The Chief turned to Ashley.

"Ms. Fontaine, I'll drive you down to the hospital myself. We'll follow the ambulance."

After more protestations and sobbing from Ashley, the Chief convinced Ashley to get into the RGPD squad car. The car slowly pulled away from the curb, not far behind the slow-moving ambulance.

Beck, Chloe, and I had barely gone back into The Laughing Loaf to catch our breath, when Mayor C came running from City Hall across the street, a look of urgency on her face.

"The Chief just called me and told me the baker for the

sourdough class died." She searched my eyes. "Gracie, what happened?"

I filled her in on the events of the morning. From the look on her face, the mayor wasn't happy that it was me filling her in and not the Chief.

"The Chief said it could be cyanide."

The mayor's eyes widened, and she shook her head. "But how? Could someone have done this during the baking class?"

I thought about the morning, from the video shoot through to the final mix of the dough, when Daniel started looking ill. I didn't know much about cyanide or how it could be administered. Several of the students had mingled with Daniel at the beginning of class, eager to meet him. Omar and Ashley had been with him from the shoot on, and both had brought him water. Could it have been in the water?

"I can't think of anyone who got close to him today except for his wife, Ashley, and his baking assistant, Omar. And Beck, of course, during the filming of the video."

The mayor looked up suddenly and connected with my eyes. "We need to take care of things since the Chief isn't here. Gracie, wrap up any leftovers carefully and put them in a safe place. They'll have to be tested." I appreciated the mayor's commitment to law enforcement, but sometimes it felt like she'd gone ahead and sworn herself in as the chief's deputy.

Beck and I had prepared the snacks, and I'd made the sourdough starter cookies this morning. I hadn't seen anyone messing with them, but then my eyes weren't constantly on the snacks or the cookies. I hadn't seen Daniel take any of the cookies, but Omar had taken quite a few. I had seen how Night Rose's employees felt about their boss.

Had Omar decided to kill his boss—by somehow poisoning one of my cookies?

"Gracie." The mayor interrupted my thoughts, waving her hand in front of my face.

"Let's go inside and have a look around the baking room."

As I opened the door to The Laughing Loaf, the Chief's actual deputy, Brad Castro, screeched up to the curb in his pickup truck.

He jumped out and ran up to us.

The young part-time deputy and Best Buy employee wore his Metallica t-shirt. "Gracie, I just got off work in Santa Cruz. The Chief told me to come directly here and talk to you."

Brad frowned as the mayor followed us to an empty table in the dining area. I took a seat.

"Mayor C, the Chief told me to talk to Gracie." He looked up at Mayor C nervously. "I need to interview her. *Alone.*"

"I was trying to step in and bring leadership during a time of crisis, Brad." Mayor C gave him a scowl, then grabbed her coffee and headed for the door.

Brad pulled a digital tablet out of his bag and tapped it to life. He set it down in front of him and looked up at me. "The Chief told me a little on his way to the hospital, but he was in a hurry, so I'll need you to fill me in. Who's the victim?"

"His name's Daniel Bordleman." I took a deep breath. I realized that I hadn't sat down all day, and I was exhausted and a little shaky from what had just happened. "He's a baker from Sonoma who came down to teach a sourdough class at The Laughing Loaf. He's also a YouTube celebrity—"

Brad's eyes lit up. "Wait. Do you mean that horror movie guy? His videos are crazy. Briana, my girlfriend, loves him."

"That's the guy." I nodded. "I met him up in Sonoma when Nate and I were up there. He agreed to teach a class at the bakery today and tomorrow. He and his wife Ashley rented a place up on Oceanview for the weekend. Between the Schiffers' and the Baxters' places."

Beck brought me a latte, and I flashed her a look of thanks.

"Then he, Ashley and Omar, one of their bakers, showed up this morning. Daniel wanted to shoot one of his videos here." I told Brad how they'd set up the back room for their horror-themed baking demonstration.

Brad typed notes onto the tablet's onscreen keyboard, while I sipped my latte and started to calm down from the day's shocking events.

"So the Chief said it looks like the guy was poisoned."

I told him about Daniel's odd color—after he changed from his Frankenstein's monster video costume, to the very end, when he sat slumped in his car, a bright shade of pink.

"I'll need the list of attendees and their contacts, Gracie."

"Why don't you come with me to the baking room," I said, getting up from my seat. Brad walked with me and started looking around the room. I'd hastily wrapped up the cookies and remaining snacks in plastic wrap on a small table near the back door. Brad snapped photos of the snacks. Then I bagged them in a black trash bag and labeled it with a Post-it note: DO NOT TOUCH!!!

My bakery was a crime scene. It felt strange. But it wasn't the first time. I wondered how we'd manage this.

Would the bakery have to be shut down while a forensics team went over it?

"These will have to be tested," Brad said, shaking his head. "If there's poison involved."

I found the attendee list on my computer and quickly printed it out. I had Ashley's phone number on my phone and the Night Rose general bakery number. I wrote them both on the class roster.

We returned to our table to talk.

"What do you know about this Daniel?" Brad asked. "Any idea who could have done this to him?"

I raised my eyebrows. "There are quite a few people who had problems with him. He wasn't well liked at his bakery. Nate and I saw that when we visited last week." I felt a sudden jab, missing Nate. "Daniel didn't treat his employees well. And judging by how his wife acted that morning, she didn't get along very well with him either."

"You mean Ashley? The woman who was here with him today?" Brad looked surprised. He typed into his tablet.

"They'd had a big argument that morning at their bakery in Sonoma. Then she plowed out the door angrily and almost ran into me."

"So Ashley Fontaine, his wife, and Omar Brightman, from his bakery—" Brad pulled out the list of contacts I'd given him "—two people who might have had cause to kill him. And they were both here today."

"Is Omar still here?" Brad asked.

"I just saw him outside by Ashley's car."

"Anybody else you can think of?" Brad typed notes into his tablet.

"Daniel seemed to have at least a friendship with one other person I'd invited to the class today. Another YouTuber. He reviews bakeries. Marco Bardugo."

Brad pulled up the piece of paper I'd printed out, with the names of the attendees.

"Got it. I will check him out. Thanks, Gracie." He looked up from the paper, an odd expression on his face. "Oh, and you're not gonna be happy with this."

I felt a sick feeling in my stomach. I had a feeling I knew what it was.

"The Chief told me you're going to have to close up the bakery. Forensics will need to go through to look for traces of cyanide if that's what killed Daniel. I mean, we don't know whether he was poisoned at the bakery or not. Then— you'll probably need to have the place professionally cleaned."

I leaned back in the chair and let out a long sigh. "Of course. It has to be safe for us to start baking again."

Brad scratched the back of his neck. "Really sorry, Gracie."

I thought about lost revenue. Hopefully that nice bump in sales from the Winter Pastry Fest would at least cushion the blow.

Brad got up and went outside to look for Omar.

THE CHIEF CAME BACK from the hospital around 2 p.m.

He pulled Beck and I aside in the dining area and asked us about the day's events. I told him what I'd seen at Night Rose up in Sonoma and what Maeve and Rafal had told me about Daniel—and Ashley.

"Crime scene will search the rental unit up on Ocean-view Drive, too, to see what they can find." The Chief sipped from his water bottle. "They're doing tests to see if he has cyanide in his system. If he does, the pathologist thinks because it took longer to have an effect, it was prob-ably in something he ate or drank."

He scrolled through messages on his phone.

"Gracie, is Nate around? I'd like to ask him a few ques-tions about what he witnessed at the bakery in Sonoma."

I kept my face a blank. If I showed any emotion here, the Chief would ask questions. I didn't want to talk about Nate's absence.

"He left for a shoot in Oregon. He should be back in about a week."

"Huh. Well, maybe I'll try to give him a call."

Beck and I stayed into the afternoon, trying to do as much damage control as possible. I put an explanation on The Laughing Loaf website's main page that we'd be closed at least through Monday. Beck, of course, made one of her very artistic signs for the front door announcing the closure. It managed to make the closure look like fun.

Nothing about it was fun.

Without my routine at the bakery, I was going to have a hard time figuring out what to do with myself for the next couple of days.

Chapter Fourteen

At 3 p.m., I drove over from my house to meet the two-person crime scene team at The Laughing Loaf.

I brought Biga with me in the car, so once I let the two technicians in, I took Biga out of his crate, snapped on his leash, and headed out for a nice long walk, since I didn't have anything better to do.

It wasn't rainy today, but the trail along the river would be muddy from the week's rains. Biga would need a bath after this, which he'd hate.

I decided to walk up Oceanview, which would take us up into the hills, but in a slower, less painful way than the route I usually drove to Elana's. It was a gradual incline, and I would pass the Baxters' house first, allowing me to skip the portion of the street with Elana's house. I missed my friend but was not in the mood to run into her.

Gradual incline or no, I still had to stop halfway up the hill to catch a breath and guzzle from my water bottle. Biga decided this was the perfect place to do his circular gotta-poop dance, so I got an even longer rest.

Scotty Baxter, River Grove's legendary 1986 chili cookoff champion, spotted me as I approached his house. He was in his front yard, a rambling space planted with large, flowering plants that resembled a small jungle and bloomed occasionally with no rhyme or reason. Most plants were dormant for the winter, but there were a couple of camellia bushes, glowing with big, white blowsy blossoms.

"Gracie! Good to see you."

I crossed the street with Biga and went up to give the frail white-haired man a big hug.

"I haven't seen you in months, Scotty. What are you up to these days?"

"Working on the yard. I'm planting bulbs for the spring. Your friend Elana came over and helped me yesterday. So we'll have a nice crop of daffodils right over here." He walked over to a patch of smoothed-over earth that ran in a haphazard row along the front porch.

"That'll be lovely," I said. I wonder if Elana knew Daniel was dead. She'd left before Ashley and Daniel had gone to their car. But I'm sure word had gotten round town pretty fast. Judging by her love for Night Rose, she'd be pretty upset about it.

"Griff enjoyed the bread class," Scotty looked up at me from behind a plowed-up row of dirt. "Too bad about that baker. Heart attack? Stroke or something like that?"

I didn't want to confirm the possibility of yet another murder in town.

"He got sick pretty quickly after class. He died right after he left the bakery."

"So what happens to all that bread dough?"

I laughed because it was such an honest question.

"The bakery's closed today while the investigators search for any environmental causes for Daniel's death." I tried to say it in neutral terms. "We've had to throw the dough out."

Scotty shook his head. "Boy. That'll make Griff real sad. He's been trying hard to bake bread."

"Scotty, please tell him I'll come over sometime and help him make a loaf when this is all over with."

"That's kind of you, Gracie." Scotty smiled and nodded as he patted down the dark earth on the row. Then he sat back on his heels and looked around, confused. "Did I just plant tulips in my daffodils?"

I smiled as I surveyed the disarray that was the Baxter front yard.

"I think whatever comes up in the spring will fit in your front yard just fine, Scotty."

He chuckled. "Well, maybe you're right, Gracie. I really don't feel like digging it up anyway."

As we prepared to leave, Biga had a quick meet and greet with Scotty's too-friendly Great Dane, Hercules, who resembled a Bengal tiger. Biga was more than ready to take the big dog on, since in his mind, he was the same size. When I heard a growl rumble from my little chihuahua mix, I tugged him away and back to the street.

If we walked on the right side of the street, I could take a look at Daniel's rental house to see if the crime scene team had arrived yet—and still stay clear of Kirk and Elana's glass-fronted split-level home a half a block down.

After listening to the Chief and doing some research online, I knew that cyanide administered in oral form killed more slowly; other forms, like cyanide gas, tended to kill instantly. Sadly, there were antidotes that could have possibly saved Daniel's life, if he'd been able to take one in time.

I wondered what time that day he'd been poisoned. I

truly hoped he hadn't been poisoned at my bakery. It was possible that he was poisoned at the rental. I was curious to see where Daniel and Ashley had been staying anyway.

As I kept right, I stepped into the yards of some of the houses, making sure I stayed out of Elana's line of sight.

Then I saw it—the large rental unit Daniel had stayed in. It could have been designed by the same architect as the Schiffers' home. The front was paneled with floor-to-ceiling windows, giving its residents a beautiful view of the hillside, with a glimpse of the ocean, and a dramatic sunset over the water if the fog lifted. Daniel and Ashley must have paid a high price for two nights in the place, even with reduced winter rates.

Not seeing any cars in the driveway, or parked nearby on the street, I walked with Biga up the concrete path, lined neatly with drought-tolerant plants and rock beds. I'd let the crime scene team into the bakery less than an hour ago. If it was the same team, I'd probably have some time before they headed up the hill to comb through the rental. I wasn't confident I could—or should—get inside, but I could certainly do my best to snoop around.

Pulling my sleeve down over my hand to avoid leaving fingerprints, I turned the knob on the front door. No luck.

Then I looked inside the large window panel next to the door—the same type of window and entrance as Elana's house down the street. The place looked tidy and spacious, with modern, minimalist furniture and floors of smooth, grey tile. A small suitcase sat in the entryway, near the door. Either Daniel and Ashley had never gotten a chance to unpack, or maybe they'd packed up items to take with them to the bookstore for Daniel's signing at the bookstore in Santa Cruz.

When I looked down, I saw dried muddy footprints

from a man's treaded shoes on the concrete. Were these from Daniel? Or the Chief or Brad had already come in and done their search this morning before I'd gotten here.

Biga was sniffing around the porch—not for clues or anything helpful, just for the usual food.

"C'mon, Biga." I tugged on the leash and headed for the walkway to the back of the house. Houses up here didn't all have fences and gates, so we were able to walk back to the wooden deck and back entrance of the rental. In the middle of the deck, outdoor chairs and a table sat ready for a picnic, aside from being covered by plastic tarps, where water from the rains had pooled.

The back door was a double French door, and I looked through the panes to a kitchen and dining area.

If the front door had been locked, maybe the crime scene team—or Daniel and Ashley themselves—hadn't been so careful with the back door.

I did my pull-down-my-sleeve trick and turned the knob on the backdoor. I slowly turned it all the way and opened the door. Biga looked up at me, skeptical.

"Come on, Biga. Don't give me that judgy look."

I took a deep breath as I walked into the kitchen. The house had the stuffy, new carpet smell of a place that rarely saw renters. A pizza box from RG's sat on the kitchen table, opened and empty, next to a bottle of red wine and two glasses, one empty, one half full. What if the wine had been poisoned? Maybe Daniel had finished his, but Ashley had delayed drinking hers, perhaps avoiding her dose of cyanide.

It didn't look like the crime scene team had been here. I was seeing the house as it was after Ashley and Daniel had left to come to The Laughing Loaf for the video filming and class.

The sink was empty, but a wrapped loaf of bread from Night Rose sat on the counter, on a cutting board. I took a look at the fridge and saw a bottle of white wine and some wrapped cheeses and lunchmeat from a deli in Santa Cruz. Biga's tail wagged when he caught sight of the food. I'd have to watch my little scavenger dog to make sure he didn't do his usual trick of licking up crumbs from the floor.

"Dude. I can't give you any of this. For all I know, everything here could be poisoned."

Biga sat down and whimpered. I plunged a hand into my purse and found five liver treats wrapped in a plastic bag. He gobbled them from my hand, and it seemed to satisfy him.

I picked up Biga and made my way to the stairs. If this house was a copy of Elana's, there would be three bedrooms upstairs. Kirk had turned one of them into an office, where he'd done much of his work during the pandemic. One was the master bedroom for him and Elana, and the third was a guest room.

Biga and I headed up the staircase, made of minimalist wooden planks. We turned into the master bedroom, where the California King-sized bed was an unmade jumble of sheets, a comforter, and discarded clothes. Socks and shirts spilled out of a suitcase opened on the love seat. All of it looked like Ashley and Daniel had unpacked and pulled out what they needed in a hurry.

On a nightstand next to the bed, there was a leather folio. I sat down on the bed. I didn't want my fingerprints to show up on a crime scene report, so I slipped on the only thing I could find in my purse—a pair of winter gloves. I carefully opened the folio. The front pocket held a printed copy of what looked like Daniel's planned remarks at the bookstore, with his notes scribbled in. It already sounded like Daniel, with overblown references to his "establishing a higher level of flavor" and "redefining bread for the next generation."

As I leafed through the pages, an unlined index card fell out of the folio. I picked it up and tried to read the lines scrawled on it in felt pen.

YOU WILL PAY FOR
WHAT YOU'VE DONE.
IT WILL COME
WHEN YOU LEAST EXPECT IT.

The words sent a shiver through me. I pulled out my phone and took a photo of it. Then I dropped the card back into the folio as if it were on fire and closed it. If the crime scene team would be coming through, they needed to see this. I had no right to take it. Well, of course, I had no right to be in this house.

This card was proof that yet another person was angry with something Daniel had done—and was threatening to take action.

"Okay, Biga. Let's get out," I whispered. I picked him up and held him, as I headed quietly toward the hallway and the stairs. Somehow finding the card had made me feel the presence of someone, someone full of anger. Someone angry enough to kill.

In my mind, I saw Rafal—as he'd described the shock of Daniel firing him. And the look he had on his face when Daniel scorned his knife work in front of visitors at the bakery.

I was halfway down the stairs when I heard a door open. There was a gust of wind coming in from outdoors, then the door closed with a rattle of panes. The back French door we'd come in. There was someone standing in the kitchen. Biga began winding up his low growl, and I clamped my hand around his mouth and whispered to him.

"Shush, Biga. Hold on."

I ducked down at the bottom of the stairs and darted into the open pantry next to the stairs. Biga was squirming, and I could feel the rumble of a growl escalating in his throat. He wanted to defend us, attack this intruder. Even though in this situation, we were the intruders. Was this the crime scene team? Or maybe Ashley. I barely breathed, trying to be absolutely silent. I couldn't wait until this person left, so we could leave, too.

The person wore boots and began to walk slowly through the kitchen area, just feet away from us. My heart pounded so hard it felt like it must be visibly shaking my chest.

Biga was about to let loose a growl. I bent down over him, covering him with my body to muffle any sound. I huddled behind the pantry's open door.

After Biga calmed down, I raised my head and looked out into the kitchen.

I gasped when I saw the face.

Chapter Fifteen

Elana looked at me with surprise.

Her face was pale. She wore gloves—which meant she was probably here for the same thing I was.

"Gracie!"

Biga squirmed in my arms, then I let him down and he immediately began panting and wagging his tail excitedly at my former friend.

"Elana, what are you doing in Daniel's rental?" How could I not be curious?

Elana looked nervous and a little guilty. "I was walking by, and I knew this was where he was staying. I thought—well, I thought I'd check around his place to see if I could find anything out."

I wasn't sure how much Elana knew about the circumstances of Daniel's death.

"Nobody's saying anything," she said, frustration in her voice. "I asked the Chief when I saw him downtown, but he said he wasn't at liberty to say. Was it murder? On the news, they just said Daniel Bordleman passed away unexpectedly.

They said the police were investigating—to see whether the death was suspicious or not."

"Elana, did you notice anything about Daniel's appearance in class?"

She raised an eyebrow. "What do you mean? He did look tired. I guess—he looked a little flushed. I thought it was because you'd turned up the heat in the room."

"The Chief's looking at the possibility that he died of cyanide poisoning." I watched as Elana picked up Biga, who began nuzzling her face.

Elana stared at me, shaking her head. "Poisoning? But why? Daniel was such a great guy. Who would do that to him?"

I frowned. "Well, you'd be surprised. When Nate and I went up to Sonoma, we saw a different side of Daniel. He was a great baker but not necessarily a great person."

I told her what Nate and I had seen at Night Rose, and what Maeve and Rafal had told me.

"Some of that makes sense, from what Kirk and I saw on our last trip up there." She stood in thought. "Something was off. I think more so on this trip. Daniel was always nice to us, since we were regulars. But he was distracted this past time. Worried about something."

I pulled my phone out of my purse.

"You know me, Elana. I have to poke my nose in things."

A smile flashed across her face then quickly disappeared.

I showed her the photo of the card with the threat on it.

She took the phone and squinted down at the photo. "Holy crap. It looks like someone carried through on their threat."

"Maybe," I said. "The thing is, lots of people had problems with Daniel. So who was it?"

We poked around the dining room and living room of the rental, trying to keep from disturbing anything or leaving signs of our presence. My winter gloves didn't help with my manual dexterity but did keep me from leaving prints everywhere.

We avoided touching plates or cups, anything Daniel might have eaten or drunk from, since they could be poisoned. Elana picked up a couple of grocery and hardware store receipts from the dining table and examined them.

The messy rental looked like Daniel and Ashley had been in a hurry, getting takeout, throwing together what they needed for the video shoot and class, then getting the heck out.

"Quick look upstairs?" I called over to Elana.

"Of course."

I picked up Biga and carried him up the stairs.

I'd already checked out the master bedroom, but I hadn't gone into the bathroom or other bedrooms.

"We need to search the bathroom," Elana said with an air of authority, heading into the master bedroom and bath. "That's where the secrets usually are."

There was an open makeup bag and a black zip-up bag sitting on the counter next to the sink.

Gingerly, I peered into the makeup bag and looked at a jumble of face cleaners and moisturizers,. The black bag was filled with a generous collection of pill bottles.

"This doesn't feel right. I feel like we're invading their privacy," I said doubtfully, as Elana examined Daniel's toiletries.

Elana held up a pill bottle triumphantly. It had DANIEL BORDLEMAN on the label. "Alprazolam," she said, reading the label. "That's Xanax. Anti-anxiety meds."

She picked up a bottle that wasn't from a pharmacy. "This looks like an over-the-counter sleeping aid."

"Which makes sense for how Daniel acted when we saw him up in Sonoma. He was stressed. He looked like he hadn't been sleeping. C'mon, Elana. It's no crime. A lot of people take these."

After the bathroom, we checked out the smaller bedrooms on either side of the master bedroom. They looked untouched. Perfectly made beds, neatly stacked books on white IKEA bookshelves. Children's décor on the walls.

WE WERE MAKING another round through the master bedroom when Elana stopped suddenly.

"Wait," she whispered. "Did you hear that?"

I stood still, listening.

Then I heard it, too. A car had pulled into the driveway. Probably the crime scene team. We stared at each other. Biga looked on the alert, like he was preparing for a full-on barking session. That would not be good.

"Elana, let's get out. Now."

I picked Biga up and put my hand around his mouth. He let out a deep, low growl. We made our way down the stairs. We headed for the back door, just as we heard a car door slam shut out front. Elana pulled the French doors shut, then we scampered across the deck and into the neighboring house's backyard, where we tried to catch our breath.

As we hid in the neighbor's overgrown backyard, with me trying to muzzle any barks from Biga, I heard a man's voice, talking on a cell phone.

"I'll be back later. I've got something to take care of."

Through the weeds, I saw a lanky man with overgrown

sandy brown hair and a down jacket heading for the back door of the rental.

This wasn't the crime scene team. It was Koa Wilson, from the class—from the vegan bakery in Eureka.

"Do you hear that?" I asked Elana in a low voice. "Can you see him?"

Elana stopped and looked over at the rental backyard, where Koa stood on the deck, scrolling through his phone. He tried the back door, which we'd locked when we'd left. When he couldn't open it, he stomped off.

"That's Koa," I whispered. "He was at your table in the class today."

Koa continued along the path to the driveway and his car.

"Bandana man? Why is he here?" Elana looked at me.

After Koa drove away, we quickly darted down to the street, through the grassy area between the houses.

We headed to the curb and continued down Oceanview.

Elana searched my face anxiously as we paused for a minute to catch our breath. "We're almost at our house. We need to talk about things, Gracie. Can you—will you come in?"

"Sure. I've got the time."

For the two months, I'd been careful to avoid Elana. Now she was inviting me over to her house. It's like I'd fallen asleep in a movie at the part where everything was messed up, then woke up again once everything had been resolved. I mean, it wasn't resolved. Elana and I needed to talk about what had happened back in October at the River-side. But at least she seemed willing to.

Kirk's mouth fell open in surprise when I walked into the dining room of their house with Elana, but he put down his spatula and came over to give me a hug. The air smelled tantalizingly of bacon and French toast. My stomach rumbled loudly, and I was hoping Kirk and Elana didn't hear it. Between my house, the bakery, and my walk up here, I hadn't had any food.

"It's good to see you, Gracie." He said warmly, as he set another spot for me at their kitchen table. I took a seat, my legs shaking a bit, because this felt surreal. Biga was sitting down next to Kirk, looking up at him as he cooked, calmly waiting for a handout.

As Kirk brought dishes over to the table, there was a sweet haze of familiarity over our gathering. I didn't think this could happen. I wanted to cry.

"Thanks for the food. I don't think I've eaten anything today."

Kirk and Elana said, in unison, "Yeah, we could tell."

I smiled and felt my eyes water up. I'd missed these people.

After the meal, Elana and I cleared the table and loaded up the dishwasher.

"Like minds, both of us heading for Daniel's rental today." I said as I settled cups into the top rack. "Since the crime scene team's been going through the bakery and we're closed today, I thought I'd look for something at the house, some clue as to what happened to Daniel."

Elana started up the dishwasher. She laid a hand on my arm. "I've got some prosecco left over from last night. Can I pour you a glass? Let's go talk."

We took glasses of the chilled sparkling wine into the living room, a room with floor-to-ceiling windows. Even on cloudy, foggy days, it felt light and airy. Like sitting outside but with the convenience of heat, air conditioning and comfy couches.

"Your house is the same model as Daniel's rental, right?" I asked Elana.

She settled herself into the loveseat and took a sip of prosecco. "Yes, and I've been wanting to see it forever. Of course, I wanted to get some answers about Daniel. Well, maybe also check out the decorating. Nice of somebody to leave the back door unlocked."

I imagined Ashley rushing out of the house Saturday morning, lugging her suitcase and props.

This felt like the comforting rhythm of Elana's and my friendship: shooting the breeze about the latest crime in town. While drinking really good wine.

"Elana, we need to talk about what happened in October. That really hurt me."

She looked down into her glass and closed her eyes. She was quiet for a while. "That night at the Riverside when the Russians were after you—that was just weird, Gracie. I was so scared. I don't know what we would have done without Reggie and his staff getting us out of there safely. I was right there with you, trying to help you. You knew why the agents were there—but you wouldn't tell me why. You told me a story that sounded totally made up. I felt like you were lying to me. I didn't know what to think."

I broke out in a sweat, remembering that night. But now I tried to imagine it through Elana's eyes.

"I had no idea you'd be dragged into it. I'm sorry for that."

"We were good friends, Gracie. I shared so much of my life with you—my marriage and my job troubles. You'd talk about Nate sometimes or what was happening at the bakery, but at a certain point, you'd just shut down. Little did I know that you had all this drama going on in your life.

I still don't get it. We were hiding out with two dangerous men after us."

She threw her hands up in frustration. "Why couldn't you tell me what was going on? Are you legally not allowed to? Are you in a witness protection program?"

I sat still, feeling sweat trickle down my back. I needed to walk a careful line. How much could I say?

"Yes," I said quietly.

Her face was getting flushed with the alcohol, and she leaned forward in the loveseat, setting her wine glass down on the coffee table. She shook her head.

"What did you just say?"

"Yes."

"Get out of town, girl." She narrowed her eyes and studied my face. "You are serious. You're in witness protection."

I widened my eyes. "I'm not supposed to talk about it. You're my friend. If I could tell you, I would."

This could be tough. One thing I knew about Elana: She hated not being in the loop—which, admittedly, I could relate to. The look on her face told me her interest had been piqued and she wanted to know even more now. What exactly had happened in my past? I'd told her about my bad partner—what was he like?

I felt shaky. I took a gulp of prosecco for reinforcement.

She looked down at her hands. "When you were away in Sonoma, I asked the Chief about you. I thought maybe you'd been in trouble with the law. Or you were one of those people who cuts a deal with a judge to give information so they get off easy."

I tried to keep from groaning in frustration. "A plea deal. What the heck, Elana."

She shook her head calmly. "No, the Chief told me you

weren't. He said you were in a bad situation, and it wasn't your fault."

This wasn't the first time the Chief had been an unexpected ally. I still didn't know how much he knew about my witness protection status, but he must know something.

"I'm sorry, Gracie." There was sadness in her eyes. "I meant to talk to you, but that night at the Riverside really shook me. I wasn't sure we'd make it out of the saloon alive. Then later, when I realized none of this had been your fault, I didn't know what to say," she said, wiping tears from her eyes with a napkin.

"My job has been pretty insane lately, but I kept looking for a chance to talk to you. I thought if I took the sourdough class maybe we could talk afterwards. I was in shock when I heard about Daniel's death after I left. When I saw you at the rental—it was like fate or the universe had intervened. Or maybe it's just that we're both snoopy people. I was just so glad to see you."

My throat tightened. "Me, too." Though I felt sad that it took someone's death to get Elana and I talking.

"Why do you think bandana man from class showed up at the rental?" Elana said, playing with the stem of her wine glass.

I threw up my hands. "No clue. I don't know much about him. He came all the way down from Eureka. I saw him try to talk to Daniel after class, but Daniel gave him a disgusted look and turned away."

"Could he have been involved somehow?" Elana asked, thinking out loud. "Then there were all those people at Night Rose who were unhappy with Daniel. What if they took advantage of his trip down to River Grove to kill him? A murder out of town would take attention off them."

"It would be hard for any of the employees to take time

off to come down here and kill their boss," I said. "I get the feeling they're running Night Rose with a skeleton crew. Their absence would be noticed."

"Unless they were all in on it," Elana said with a knowing look. "Like in Agatha Christie's *Murder on the Orient Express*."

"Interesting theory." I nodded, with a half-smile. As much as I missed Nate, it was more fun hashing this out with Elana. "Night Rose's employees all seemed to feel the same way about Daniel."

The only one I wasn't sure of was Omar. I'd heard Rafal's story, but from what I saw at today's class, Omar seemed to be able to work with Ashley and Daniel just fine.

I took another swig of prosecco, "Cyanide is such a bizarre way to kill someone. It does sound like something from a 1930s murder mystery."

Elana nodded thoughtfully. "I wonder if there was some reason to do it that way. So maybe it wouldn't look like murder, more like a heart attack or natural causes."

"It might have looked like that, but one of the EMTs just happened to be familiar with the symptoms—the bright pink skin." Biga jumped up on the couch next to me, having apparently run out of things to lick off the kitchen floor. "Someone in the class or at the bakery could have done it. Or even someone earlier—at the rental house."

"Ashley, his wife," Elana said, with excitement in her voice.

Our conversation made me think of something: with Daniel dead, who was in charge of Night Rose? As his wife, Ashley might be the new owner of a very profitable bakery business. That could be motive enough for killing him. Now I wanted to find out.

The prosecco relaxed both of us, and after throwing our

theories about Daniel's murder out there, Elana poured us a second glass. We started talking about other parts of our lives. Elana was excited about a possible transfer to a better job within her company, so she could finally escape the boss from hell. She and Kirk were planning on getting a dog in the spring.

I told Elana about Nate going quiet and taking off on another shoot—almost immediately after we'd gotten back from Sonoma. When it came down to it, witness protection was brutal on my relationships.

"Gracie, thank you for telling me this," Elana said. "Nate's a good man. Maybe he needs time to think this through. That's not a bad thing."

I nodded reluctantly. "Yeah. But it hurts, especially after our getaway. We had a great time, then suddenly he pulled back."

Elana thought about this for a minute. "For Mountain Man, this is what he has to go through. Let him be out thinking in the woods with the birds if he needs to."

She was right.

Even if I wasn't sure what lay ahead for me and Nate, it looked like I had my best friend back.

After we finished off the prosecco, Kirk offered to drive me back to the bakery to get my car. Biga, having been fed, cuddled and cooed over, was not thrilled about leaving the Schiffer house. Kirk bent down and scratched his back, and Biga looked up at the man with his big round chihuahua eyes like he was begging him to keep him.

"Thanks for the dinner, Kirk." I smiled and hugged Elana and Kirk.

"You won't be at the bakery tomorrow because of the cleaners, right?" Elana looked at me hopefully. "Want to catch lunch?"

I'd planned on doing some work at home on the bakery's accounting system, something I had to do, but which would bore me to tears.

"I'd like to, but I have a few things to do. And I'm supposed to meet with the Chief. Rain check? We need to go back to the Riverside some night soon."

Elana nodded. "We need a redo." Impulsively, she reached to give me another hug. "I can't tell you how sorry I am for what happened, Gracie," she whispered. "I know this doesn't mean everything is instantly okay again. But please—can we keep talking?"

Chapter Sixteen

y the time Kirk let Biga and me off at the bakery, it was dark.

The crime scene team was packing up, its van pulled up close to The Laughing Loaf's back door. The solitary River Grove PD car was parked in the alley, next to my car. It was either the Chief or Brad, and from my knowledge of Brad's limited availability on weekends, the deputy was probably working at his second job today.

"Done already?" I greeted the two CS investigators, outfitted in protective gear, one woman in her forties and a younger man with dark hair and light blue eyes whose coloring reminded me of Nate's. It caught me by surprise, and I suddenly missed him.

"We took the food, a couple of water bottles and some samples of powder from the floor," the woman said, as she zipped up a bag and set it in the back of the van. I wondered if the white powder was flour, since there were nine people in the bakery the previous day, mixing and kneading with it. "We also went through the trash in the bin outside the bakery. The samples will all go to the lab for testing, which may take a while. As soon as we find out, Chief Westerman will let you know. After your cleaners finish up, you should be good to go.”

“Thanks. Is the Chief here? I saw his car out back.”

“He said he was going to the front of the bakery to take some calls.” The young man said.

I took Biga around with me to the front of the bakery, where I found the Chief at the usual corner table, typing something on his tablet.

“You’re not supposed to be here, Gracie.” The Chief looked up at me sternly. “Not till after the cleaners leave tomorrow.”

“I do have a vested interest in opening back up soon,” I replied. “I wanted to see how things were going. Crime scene’s packing up. They’re heading up to Daniel’s rental.”

“I had a look at the place after we finished the interviews here,” the Chief said. “Brad and I went through. We didn’t find much, though we’ll find out from the testing if there are traces of cyanide.”

“I was up that way, visiting Elana just a few minutes ago,” I said, twisting the truth a little. I wasn’t about to admit I’d been in the rental.

The Chief shook his head. “You told me Daniel wasn’t well liked by his employees. Looks like I’ll be headed up to Sonoma for some interviews.”

I hesitated to bring it up, because I did like Rafal and sympathized with his situation, which seemed unfair.

“There’s another employee, Rafal. Daniel fired him a couple of weeks ago. It caught him by surprise. He was pretty angry about it.”

“You’re not the first one to mention him,” the Chief nodded. “Ms. Fontaine told me about Daniel firing him, and said she was scared of what he might do. Omar agreed with her. We intend to find the man and question him," the Chief said, a resolute look on his face. I gave him the contact info I'd gotten from the baker when Nate and I had talked to him in Bodega Bay. I felt guilty, like I was turning Rafal in.

I thought it was interesting that both Ashley and Omar were quick to name him as a suspect.

I thought of my conversation with Elana today, as we brainstormed possible suspects.

"What do you think of Ashley Fontaine? You drove her to the hospital yesterday after Daniel's death. Since she's Daniel's wife, it's possible she inherits his bakery. That's a strong motive for murder."

The Chief gave me a grim look. "Gracie, the woman was hysterical most of the drive. I went with her because she was incoherent, in shock that her husband was dead. It didn't seem like an act to me."

"Hmmm. Okay, Chief." I nodded slowly, not hiding my skepticism. He could be right. In my experience, men tend to give a very large helping of benefit of the doubt to young, good-looking women.

"I know you'll be losing a few days of business." He leaned back in his chair. "Since you're not going to be here tomorrow, why don't you come up to Sonoma with me? If those employees already know you, it might be helpful to have you there. You spent some time with Rafal, too."

I thought about my alternatives: stay in River Grove and work on my accounting system while I waited for the cleaners to finish. Or go up to Sonoma, score some really good bread at Night Rose—and indulge my curiosity about suspects.

"I'm in, Chief."

* * *

SUNDAY, *December 15*

The next morning, as I got dressed and gulped down a homemade espresso, Biga knew something was going on. This was not our daily routine. First of all, we'd gotten up at 7:30 a.m., not 4:30 a.m. And I wasn't trying to herd him into his crate.

He followed me around as I got dressed, watching me inquisitively until finally I asked my father to distract him with a run around the back yard. As soon as my father opened the back door, Biga darted out, ready to cavort and chase squirrels. I grabbed my purse and notebook and hurried out the front door.

The Chief was waiting outside in the RGPD car. I pulled open the door, buckled in, and we were off.

The Chief was drinking a pathetic-looking cup of coffee in a styrofoam cup he'd gotten at the quickie mart on the highway just past downtown.

"I can't wait till Laughing Loaf opens again," he said with a groan. "This is the worst coffee I've ever had. Brown water, with grounds in it. I can't believe I used to drink it before you opened the bakery. Now I can't stand it."

I laughed. "That's high praise, Chief. I will pass that on to Beck."

"Now coffee is the *only* thing I can have at your bakery." He grumbled under his breath, his eyes on the road as we headed up Highway 1. The coast was socked in with fog this morning, but I'd learned to appreciate the fog in my new hometown. It blurred the landscape, turning scenery into a soft impressionist painting.

When we turned onto Bodega Highway, it started raining. Tall eucalyptus trees lining the road waved in the wet wind. We pulled into the Night Rose parking lot, where the lot was only half full. I remembered, after the past few head-spinning days, that it was Sunday, which should be one of their busiest days of the week.

It was 10:30 a.m., so the bakery had been open for a while.

Maeve Killoran was at the front counter, adding loaves to the display case from a metal cart. She looked startled to see me. Omar saw me and waved from one of the tables in the back. There were three unfamiliar bakers working at the tables.

Then I saw Ashley Fontaine coming down the stairs from the upstairs office, wearing heels and an apron which looked incongruous over a blue, almost formal dress. She didn't see us at first, but when she did, she didn't look happy.

"You're Maeve Killoran?" The Chief asked the red-haired young woman, once she slid the case closed and returned to the register. "I'm Chief Dave Westerman of the River Grove Police Department. Is there a place we can talk?"

Maeve looked over at Ashley, who was approaching the counter. "We aren't very busy, so I guess—"

Ashley gave a curt nod. "Fine. Use the video room upstairs."

"I'd like to speak to you first, Ms. Fontaine." The Chief caught her eye.

Ashley's eyes widened. She gestured to the baking area behind her.

"Do you realize what I'm dealing with here after Daniel's death?" She sniffed as if she were somewhere between offended and grief stricken. "I've just taken on a lot of responsibilities. I don't have time to answer a lot of questions."

"Ashley, are you now the owner of Night Rose?" I wanted to know, though it wasn't really my job to ask.

"I am," she snapped, shooting me an angry look. "It's a huge job."

Daniel was a hands-on micromanaging boss. He probably hadn't allowed Ashley to make many management decisions at the bakery.

"I'm sure it is, Ms. Fontaine," the Chief said gently. "My sympathies for the loss of your husband. We do need to talk to you, however, as part of our investigation into his death."

One of the new bakers came up to her and pulled her aside, talking in a low, but urgent voice. I heard the words "delayed" and "shipment."

Granted, Daniel had only been dead one day, and Ashley could be dealing with some intense grief. But she seemed unprepared for her new job as owner and manager —and in over her head. I worried that, unless she hired someone on as a manager, Night Rose wouldn't last long.

"Ashley, how long have you known that you would inherit Night Rose if Daniel passed away?" I asked. I had a hard time picturing Ashley as a calculated killer, someone who'd poisoned her husband so she could own the bakery. For one thing, she seemed to have no plan in place for running it.

"We talked about it before we got married." Ashley sniffed again and rubbed her eyes. A mascara-tinged tear rolled down her cheek. "He s-said I was the only person he trusted."

Daniel did seem to have trust issues. Judging from the cookbook introduction, trust had been a problem with his former partner and employees at his previous bakeries. So he found and married someone who did exactly what he said, without question. And now she had no idea how to handle things without him.

"Ashley, when I visited Night Rose two weeks ago, I was waiting for the woodfired baking class outside. I heard you and Daniel arguing and you left in a hurry." A look of panic crossed her face. "Do you remember what that was about?"

She inclined her head and looked down at her hands. "Daniel was involved in a—a business dealing with someone. I thought it was a bad idea—maybe even dangerous. I'd just found out about it, and I told him that."

The Chief immediately looked up from his phone. "What was the business deal?"

She tucked her hair behind one ear and picked at the bright pink polish on her nails. "Daniel found out some information about someone. He thought it was funny at first. Then he said he was going to use it to see what he could get out of it."

The Chief snorted. "That sounds like blackmail to me. Was he trying to get money out of this person?"

Ashley's eyes darted away nervously. She looked like she regretted mentioning it. Her lips twitched. "How should I know?"

"You need to tell me who this person is, Ms. Fontaine," the Chief leaned forward in his chair. "Now."

"He was there at the class on Saturday," she said, her voice wavering. "His name's Marco. Marco Bardugo."

After Ashley went back downstairs, Maeve came into the video room, where we took seats around what had been Daniel's desk.

"You've worked here for how long, Ms. Killoran?"

"Three years." She pressed her lips together. "To be honest, I'm done. Ashley knows nothing about running a bakery. It was so disorganized this morning, we ended up opening two hours late. I'm turning in my notice."

I took a deep breath. "My sympathies, Maeve."

The Chief continued with his line of questioning. He probably didn't understand how jaw-dropping this was—that a bakery of Night Rose's reputation would open that late on one of its busiest days of the week.

"Can you tell me, Ms. Killoran," he began. "How did most of the Night Rose employees feel about Daniel Bordleman?"

Maeve let out a bitter laugh. "He underpaid us, overworked us, and insulted us on a regular basis in front of each other and in front of customers. He told us we were lucky to have jobs here. So none of us liked him, no."

I jumped in. "What about Omar?" I thought of Omar's friendliness toward Daniel and Ashley at the class.

"Omar went overboard to be nice to Daniel. He thought it gave him job security. I'm not sure it helped him very much. Daniel didn't treat him any better than he treated us."

The Chief looked puzzled. "If it's such a bad place to work, why did you all stay here?"

Maeve sighed heavily, repeating what she'd told me two weeks ago. "If we worked under Daniel, that experience looked great on our record. And if we tried to get another job, he could put the word out to local employers not to hire us."

The Chief pulled a piece of paper from a folder. He set it down in front of her. A printed copy of the threat I'd found in the folio in Daniel's rental.

"Ms. Killoran, can you tell me who wrote this?"

Maeve's eyes opened wide. She turned pale, high-lighting the light freckles across her nose.

"Who wrote this, Ms. Killoran?" The Chief repeated.

She shook her head and pushed back from the desk. "He was just angry because Daniel fired him, but Rafal is not that kind of person—he would never—"

"Do you know where Rafal is now?" I asked.

She put her hand to her forehead as if she were getting a headache. "He found a job. At a new pastry shop, Le Pain Parisienne. He wants to get me a job there, too."

The Chief turned to Maeve.

"Ms. Killoran, does Rafal or anyone else at Night Rose have access to cyanide?"

"Cyanide?" She looked pained, as if she was going to cry. "Is that what killed him?"

The Chief nodded. "Is there anyone you know who has access to a poison like that?'

She shook her head. "Oh, my God. How awful. No—I can't think of anyone I know who would."

After Maeve went back downstairs, the Chief and I looked at each other.

"That's more than I expected we'd get," I said.

"Something to follow-up on, anyway." The Chief said, a faint note of hope in his voice. "We need to talk to Rafal. Damn, it's going to kill me to go to that pastry shop and not get any sweets."

RAFAL's new place of employment was in downtown Napa, a tiny shop gleaming with pristine white walls, marble counters and brand-new signage. The brightly lit display case was filled with neat rows of tiny tarts, cakes, prof-iteroles, macarons and French canelés, which looked like little caramel-brown towers. Baguettes and rustic loaves in bags lined shelves behind the counter.

The smell of sweet baked goods was intoxicating. The chief took a long look at the display case like he was paying his respects to a dear friend he'd never see again.

I bought a box of tarts and canelés to bring back for Beck to sample for research.

The Chief waved over the dark-eyed young woman behind the counter, dressed in a white baking coat. "We'd like to talk to Rafal Nowak."

She nodded. "Just a minute." She went through the swinging door to the back of the shop.

Soon, Rafal came out, smiling cautiously at me. He turned pale when he saw the Chief.

"Rafal, we'd like to ask you some questions about Daniel Bordleman," the Chief looked around the small shop. "Is there a place we can talk?"

Rafal led us to a small white table outside the café, facing the street. We sat down and Rafal looked uneasy, shifting in his seat and looking out to the sidewalk and street as if he were preparing to make a run for it.

The Chief pulled out the copy of the threat found at the rental. Rafal swallowed, then turned away, as if he couldn't bear to look at it.

"You wrote this, didn't you, Rafal?" The Chief sat back in his chair and watched the baker, studying his face for a reaction.

Rafal swallowed and nodded. "Two weeks ago. I wrote it after Daniel fired me and called me bad names. Said I was a liar. When I was here from the beginning. I helped him make Night Rose what it is."

"Did you mean to carry through with the threat?" I asked.

"At the time, maybe." He shrugged. "For how he treated Maeve and all of us. Because we gave him our best to make his bakery great, and he threw it in the trash. I wanted him to be scared."

Rafal shook his head and looked down. He looked almost ashamed, but I couldn't see his eyes.

"After I saw you and your boyfriend in Bodega Bay, Gracie, I wrote the note. I went back to Night Rose at 3 a.m. and slipped it under the door in an envelope with his name on it. I knew he'd see it. He was always the first to go in. He couldn't stand any of us being there earlier than he was."

"Did you do anything else to Daniel?" The Chief studied the baker's face.

Rafal looked down at the table soberly then shook his head. "Two days after I was fired, I applied to work here. They were about to open and needed a bread baker, and I had the skills. Instead of giving them references, I baked a batch of baguettes on the spot that afternoon. They hired me right away, no questions asked. It pays the same and everyone's nice to me. I am still sad for what happened. But I have moved on from Night Rose."

There was a settled look on his face. He was trying to get Maeve a job at Le Pain Parisienne, too.

From the Chief's expression, I couldn't tell if he believed Rafal. I thought about how Rafal had run away from Nate and me in Bodega Bay. Why had he really run from us? Had he been working on some plan to kill Daniel? Maybe out hunting for the cyanide?

"Do you have access to cyanide, Mr. Nowak?" The Chief asked. "Tell me the truth."

Rafal looked the Chief directly in the eye. "No, I do not."

"Is there anyone you know who has access to cyanide?" The Chief asked.

Rafal paused for a moment then shook his head firmly. "No one."

"Where were you on Saturday, Mr. Nowak?"

Rafal looked nervous. "I was working early here—till 10 a.m. Then I was with Maeve at her place."

After a few more questions, the Chief looked at me and closed his notebook.

As THE SKY started to fill with clouds again, the Chief and I pulled off the road out of town to get coffee from a roadside drive-thru coffee spot.

The Chief took a sip and gave his verdict. "It's better than the convenience store."

It was hot, and it had caffeine and cream and sugar in it, which made it good enough for me.

I started thinking about what Ashley had said about Marco Bardugo.

"So Rafal did threaten Daniel. And he's admitted it. But if Daniel was blackmailing Marco Bardugo like Ashley said —Marco had a motive for killing him."

The Chief reached for his coffee. "All we have is Ashley's word that Daniel intended to mess with Marco. She didn't give us details about it. But we do have the facts on Rafal. He's admitted to threatening the victim and possibly intending to harm him."

"Yeah, but Marco and Daniel did have a strange interaction at the end of class. I saw it. I think it's worth finding out what Daniel knew about Marco."

The Chief sighed. "What do you recommend I do,

Gracie, go see Marco and ask him point blank—'hey, what damaging information did Daniel know about you?'"

I snorted. "That's where we need to do some research."

"If you want to pursue that, why don't you just go ahead." The Chief said with smugness in his voice.

"Thanks, Chief. Maybe I will." I smugged him right back.

I pulled out my phone and checked it.

"I'm hoping to get a text soon that the bakery is good to go." If it was fully cleaned and ready, I'd set up scones in the freezer and mix cinnamon roll dough for an overnight rise. Beck and I could pull everything else together in the morning.

Soon we were back on Highway 101 South, as bright green hills rolled by on our right. The rains had turned them a stunning sap green, even greener than they'd been when Nate and I had come to Sonoma for our getaway. I sighed and leaned my head against the headrest. It had been almost a week since Nate had left for his shoot in Oregon.

No calls, not even any texts with recordings of bird calls. Maybe Elana had been right: Nate needed his time to think about things. To think about whether he could deal with me and my witness protection life. I had to accept his decision, even if it wasn't the decision I wanted.

In the meantime, I had to get my mind off my problems. I wanted to get back to the comforting daily routine of the bakery, the smells of cinnamon rolls in the morning, and the happy chatter of customers.

That bakery better be open for business soon.

Chapter Seventeen

I got the text just as we crossed the Golden Gate Bridge.

All finished, Gracie. Locked up. Key's in mail slot.

Now I was in a better mood. It was 3 p.m., and we'd be home by 4:30 even with traffic, according to the GPS app on my phone. I'd have an early dinner at home with my dad, then head for the bakery. I texted Beck. If she wanted to work on beignets or tarts this evening, she could join me.

OMG. YES!!!!!!

Followed by a high-five emoji and multiple smileys with hearts for eyes.

I laughed.

"Chief, we're back in business."

"Great to hear, Gracie," the Chief said as we made our

way through San Francisco. "I know where I'm getting my coffee tomorrow morning."

WHEN I CAME through the front door of my house, Biga tackled me with all twelve pounds of furry fury, his tail wagging. Then he proceeded to stalk me as I walked through the house, to make sure I didn't ever leave again.

My dad was in his study. I poked my head in. He was absorbed in a YouTube documentary on physicist Werner Heisenberg. I wondered, being a little snarky, if he had long talks with Mary Jo Hartman on the principles of theoretical physics.

"Early dinner okay? The cleaners finished up and Beck and I need to do prep for tomorrow."

Without taking his eyes off of the computer screen, he gave me a distracted nod.

"Sure, dear."

I rooted through the fridge and found shredded chicken and a salad mix. I made a chicken salad with cannellini beans and roasted red peppers. Then I toasted some sourdough slices, slathering them with basil walnut pesto I'd made earlier in the week.

I poked my head into his office and pulled him away from his fascinatingly esoteric lecture to eat.

"How were the interviews?" My father asked as he followed me back to the kitchen. "No arrest yet?"

"Nope." I took my seat at the table and bit into my pesto toast with a loud crunch. "There are a couple of suspects. A former baker at Night Rose who the chief thinks did it. The other, a YouTube bakery reviewer, might have been blackmailed by Daniel."

"Just what you needed, more people to add to the list," my dad said with a smirk.

"Now it's a matter of who was with Daniel that day, and how he was given the cyanide—which had to happen sometime that morning. For that, it seems like Ashley makes most sense, since she was with him. But then, any of the students or Omar, theoretically, could have done it."

I took a sip of white wine and speared a forkful of salad.

"Ashley did inherit Night Rose—a great motive for murder. The Chief and I interviewed her today.But if she killed him for the bakery, she had no plan for running it. She's overwhelmed. I'm not sure she even wants it at this point."

"Do you agree with the Chief that the baker did it, dear?"

"Rafal was angry," I said. "He even admitted he wanted to hurt Daniel. But he's in a much better situation now with a new job—and a girlfriend. I don't think he felt like killing Daniel by the time Saturday's class rolled around."

"It seems quite simple to me," my father said, with a satisfied smile. "The poisoning had to happen that morning at the class. All things being equal—out of everyone who hated Daniel—find whoever had closest access to him during that time. You're a smart one, Gracie. Figure it out." In my father's mind the subject was wrapped up. He started in on his salad.

"Sure, that's easy. Why didn't I think of that?" I groaned at him.

My father took a drink from his water glass. "Why don't you see if the class was filmed?"

I laid down my fork and stared at him. *Damn.*

I ran to get my phone to text the Chief.

The Chief texted back a few minutes later that he was

trying to get a search warrant for Night Rose, to find the video recording of the class, if Ashley had recorded it. He'd keep me posted.

Feeling bad for Biga's separation anxiety, I took Biga with me to the bakery after dinner. He actually seemed happy to be there, and certainly excited to see Beck. We both played with him in his pen, cuddling with him and taking turns making him do tricks for treats. Then we scrubbed our hands and started the baking prep for tomorrow.

Every square inch of the place had been cleaned and wiped down. The tables where eight bakers had worked on Saturday were sparkling clean, no trace of flour. We'd had to get rid of all the tubs of dough, as well as the students' jars of starters. The oven had been cleaned out and the sides, bottom and racks shone like new. Fresh fruit and herbs, along with all the contents of the refrigerators and my sourdough starter tub, had been thrown out, which made me sad; luckily, a bakery owner in San Jose was donating a batch of their fed starter. Sympathetic to our situation, he'd volunteered someone to drop it off tomorrow morning, so we'd be able to bake sourdough loaves later this week.

Beck turned on the music for the evening, choosing a power pop playlist. She danced in place as she rolled out a batch of crust dough for the tarts. I mixed up a double batch of cinnamon roll dough in the big stand mixer, since it was supposed to be especially cold tomorrow morning.

"Does the Chief have any suspects?" Beck asked, sweetly digging for information. "If you went up to Sonoma today, he must have somebody in mind."

"We interviewed a few Night Rose employees." I shrugged. "I think the Chief and I have very different ideas about who might have done it."

"That's happened before, hasn't it?" She grinned.

"Yep. Every time."

I mixed batches of brioche and sourdough and slid the tubs into the proofer. Then I unlocked the storeroom to see if I had anything I could add to a batch of scones. Nobody had access to the locked room during the class, so ingredients in the room remained untouched during the search by the CSI team and then the cleaners.

In the storeroom, I found a bag of dried currants I'd never used. Orange zest would be a nice complement, but I had no oranges to add some complexity to the flavor. In my imagination, Daniel appeared, wild-eyed, his hands waving as he lectured me about my boring mix of flavors and lack of fresh ingredients.

I mixed up a batch of currant scones, grated frozen butter over the dough, and began rolling it out, as Beck mixed her beignet dough. Soon I had five trays of laminated currant scones in the freezer to bake up tomorrow morning.

We prepped our way through at least two playlists, and it felt so good to be back in the bakery again with Beck. Tomorrow the bakery would open at 7:00 a.m. as usual. We wouldn't be fully stocked, but we would be ready for business.

I couldn't wait.

We were still singing on our way out to our cars after locking up.

Chapter Eighteen

When I got home, it was 8:30 p.m.

I got a text from Elana asking if I wanted to go to The Riverside for dinner tomorrow night. There was a jazz funk band from New York playing that she wanted to see. Instead of spending another night at home, staring at my phone, I needed to get out. Hopefully this evening at The Riverside would end better than our last outing.

I responded.

YES!

As I obsessively checked my phone, my heart began to pound. Would there be a call or text from Nate? 9 p.m. came and went with nothing. I threw on my down jacket and chased Biga around the cold backyard to get the disappointment out of my system.

I came back in and flopped down on the living room couch, with Biga curled up at my feet, ready to do some research on Marco Bardugo.

With headphones on, as my father read in his chair across from me, I watched several of Marco's review videos on YouTube. He and Daniel had a lot in common. Both were in their late 30s, had a wicked sense of humor, and turned baking into entertainment. While Daniel actually baked in his videos, Marco shot footage at bakeries and restaurants, interviewing bakers and chefs, and sampling their offerings.

Marco rated good restaurants with stars—up to five. When an establishment was truly bad, Marco was savage in his reviews, rating each place with a row of dumpsters on fire—from one dumpster to five. One restaurant in San Francisco was rated the worst, with five dumpster fires. According to Marco, the poor service and obvious health code violations earned it that rating.

As I went through the videos, I noticed that all Marco's scathing dumpster-on-fire videos had high numbers of views, some over a million. His starred reviews of bakeries, including one that mentioned Laughing Loaf favorably, earned much less—in the 200,000–400,000 view range.

People wanted to watch Marco trash bakeries and restaurants. It was entertainment.

I wondered what information Daniel had found about Marco, that might be blackmail material. Something in his past? Or something that people hurt by his harsh reviews would jump on, happy to see Marco's sins exposed.

I googled Marco Bardugo, and the only results were his YouTube videos and interviews with him in culinary magazines or by other content creators. A television station posted a story about an angry bakery owner in LA, who argued the claims in Marco's negative review were unfounded. He was planning to sue.

A Wikipedia page listed Marco's biography. He'd gone

to the Culinary Institute of America (CIA) and worked at a series of bakeries and as a pastry chef. Then at the bottom, in small print, I saw a tiny line of text. *See Mark Anton Bradley.*

Intrigued, I googled the name.

Up came a photo that looked a lot like Marco Bardugo. Except he wore a buzz cut—not the overgrown shaggy look he'd had at the class. And wire-rimmed aviator glasses. Was Marco Bardugo really Mark Anton Bradley?

There was no entry for Mark Anton Bradley on Wikipedia. There were some old Facebook posts tagged with the name, showing a skinny young man posed with his high school audiovisual club—all of them holding video cameras and recording equipment. There was a resemblance in the features, but I barely recognized the scrawny young man in the photos as the slick, leather-jacket-wearing dude who'd shown up to the sourdough class at The Laughing Loaf.

Tomorrow during the mid-morning lull at the bakery, I'd make a few phone calls.

* * *

MONDAY, *December 16*

As rain poured down outside, the bakery hummed the next morning with conversation and sounds of clinking cups and plates. A buttery cinnamon scent filled the room as customers devoured warm cinnamon rolls.

Most bakery customers were okay with our reduced menu.

Nobody complained about currant scones being boring.

Everybody asked about Daniel's death when they ordered. I got tired of answering their questions.

"No, we don't know exactly what happened, Janet. Mr. Bordleman died in his car outside the bakery. We had to close while inspectors tried to figure out if there was something in the bakery that could have triggered it."

That seemed to satisfy most customers.

Beck had fried up beignets and French toast sticks and had them ready at opening, so the high schoolers didn't notice any difference in the offerings. A few adults, however, noticed the missing items.

"So you're telling me you have no kale frittata cups." Regular customer, Rick Vega, a serial complainer, tapped impatiently on the counter as he waited for his latte. "Gracie, that's not fair to us regulars."

"We had an emergency closure and couldn't get back into the bakery till late yesterday," I said, trying to summon Beck's patience and sweetness, which didn't come naturally to me. "We had to limit our menu for today, Rick. They'll be back on the menu for tomorrow."

Since it was raining, customers hung out in the dining area longer than usual, some of them reading, some lingering and talking over coffee. A couple played a leisurely game of backgammon.

Beck had cleared off a few empty tables and was taking a full tub of cups and plates back to the dishwasher.

"Will you be okay manning the counter if I take a break and make a phone call?"

She smiled. "No problem. Everyone's just hanging out right now."

I sat down at my desk in the tiny closet office right off the back room.

I had a couple of phone numbers. One was a Kate Bradley, in the city of Manteca, California, about an hour outside of the Bay Area. She looked to be the mom of the listed Mark Anton Bradley, judging by a series of connections I made as I went through old social media accounts. The other was for the Culinary Institute of America location in Yountville, in Sonoma County. It had been mentioned in Marco Bardugo's Wikipedia listing.

I called CIA first, asking to verify whether Marco Bardugo had ever been a student there. When the woman administrator couldn't find his name in the records, I asked about Mark Anton Bradley. She didn't find any record of that name either.

He wasn't the first person to do it, but Marco Bardugo—or just Mark—had lied about his education on his resume. Was this what Daniel could have been blackmailing him about?

I didn't get back to my desk till after we closed for the day. I had to shape loaves for baking, and then we had a surge in customers wanting hot coffee and tea after lunch.

Then I called Kate Bradley on my burner phone, which I usually used for calling my witness protection agents. A young woman answered, who explained her mother was in the hospital and that she was Teresa Bradley, Kate's daughter. I told her I'd gone to high school with Mark and wanted to get in contact with him. I gave my name as Emily.

"It's been so long. I remember seeing him at work back then—now where was that place again?"

"Breakfast Boss in Modesto. He worked there for *years*," Teresa said, in a mocking tone. "Taking orders in the drive thru. Pretty funny considering what he's doing now. Like his only experience is working at a drive-thru donut shop. Oh my God, my brother is so lame. He is so full of himself."

"What do you mean?" I asked, wanting to hear her take on this. "What's Mark doing now?"

She snorted. "I'm surprised you didn't know. He's kind of a big deal on YouTube."

"What? No way." I acted completely shocked.

"He's calling himself Marco Bardugo. And now he's this reviewer on YouTube, pretending to be a food critic."

Chapter Nineteen

The Chief came over at 4 p.m., knocking on the back door from the alley, since we were closed. I let him in.

He looked interested in what I had to say, which made me hopeful that he'd started to question his theory about Rafal being the killer.

"I've been trying to track down that video of Saturday's class. Ashley claims she's been busy with the bakery and doesn't know where it is. We'll have the warrant soon."

He rubbed his eyes. It had been a tough couple of days for him. "You said you have something to tell me about the food reviewer. What's going on?"

I told him about my research into Marco Bardugo. How I'd found out that he had lied about having a culinary education; his only real experience in the food industry was a drive-thru donut shop.

"Could be a motive, I guess," the Chief said, a skeptical look on his face. "But is it really that big of a deal? He just makes videos. Somebody can't make money doing that, can they?"

I told him about how much YouTube personalities make —with the amount of followers both Daniel and Marco had, they were pulling in a good salary every month.

"If Marco was exposed as a fraud, he could lose his followers," I said.

Beck, who was more of a YouTube watcher than I was, chimed in as she filled a tray of apple tart shells.

"It's true, Chief."

The Chief shook his head. "I don't get all this computer stuff. I have to trust you two. I can't believe people make money just filming those silly videos. But if Daniel was blackmailing Marco, I need to talk to him. Whatever his name is."

After the Chief left, Beck and I finished up. I slid trays of scones into the freezer—cranberry and fresh, fragrant sage this time, which Daniel would have approved of. Beck finished up her tarts, so they'd be ready to bake tomorrow morning.

"Beck, you're more familiar with these videos than I am," I said as we prepared to lock up and leave. "If people find this out, will it end Marco Bardugo's career?"

Beck thought about this. "If he is exposed as a liar, there will be people making YouTube videos about what a scammer he is. Those videos will be the ones getting views."

* * *

As I WIPED down tables in the dining area, through The Laughing Loaf front window, I saw the Chief walk across the street to City Hall. About fifteen minutes later, Marco Bardugo opened the green door of City Hall himself—he must have still been in the area after the weekend's class. I'd love to hear the conversation between the two, but it was none of my business. The Chief would probably tell me how it went anyway.

I was meeting Elana at The Riverside tonight, after finishing up here and then freshening up and changing my clothes at home. With the stress of the case, and the absence of my boyfriend, I needed a night out.

When I pulled into our driveway, Mary Jo Hartman's bright orange VW bug was parked in front of our house. I knew my father would be enjoying himself tonight, and he'd probably invited her over after I texted him that Elana and I would be out.

I unlocked the door and went inside, to the delight of Biga, who ran to me, tail wagging.

I heard my dad in the kitchen, excitedly telling a story about the time he'd almost been knocked out in a bar fight in his hometown in Surrey. I'd heard the story many times. It was a funny story of mistaken identity that my father tended to tell when he'd had a drink or two. Mary Jo laughed so hard she started to gasp.

"Oh, John, you are so funny. I can't believe you got out of that one without a black eye."

"Hey, Dad, Mary Jo. I'm home," I poked my head into the kitchen, where my father was sitting in a chair peeling potatoes and Mary Jo had *my* cookbook open on the table in front of her.

"Gracie, good to see you, hon," Mary Jo got up and gave me a hug. She smelled of cigarettes and Juicy Fruit gum. "Your father and I are making potato soup and salad for dinner."

"That's a perfect meal for this weather," I said with a smile. "Have fun, you two, and save me some soup. Dad, I'll be back around 10-10:30. Don't forget to let Biga out in the backyard, so he can do his thing."

Biga followed me into my room, and I shut the door to get ready.

I secretly hoped Mary Jo would be gone when I came home, though I knew there was no real reason why I shouldn't want her around. She was friendly, nice to me, and she seemed to enjoy my dad—and he definitely seemed to enjoy her.

I quickly dressed in a maroon shirt and light brown corduroys and my favorite kickass suede boots. After putting on some makeup, I waited till Elana texted that she was in my driveway.

"Let's go, girl," Elana said excitedly, as she backed her Acura out of the driveway and turned to head downtown to The Riverside. "It's been a crazy week at work. Boss is on the rampage about something the CEO asked for that she swears she told me to do—and no, she didn't. I need to burn off some stress."

It was only a Monday night, but as we approached downtown, The Riverside Saloon was brightly lit and jumping. The lot out front was filled with cars. I heard the deep thump of a bass doing a walk down as we parked.

"Is this group really famous?" I asked. "It looks packed."

"This is their only West Coast performance. You know how Reggie McFerrin knows everybody. He was able to get them."

We walked into Riverside's main hall, which was rapidly filling up.

"This is just the warm-up band," Elana waved her hand dismissively. "It's early yet."

"It's quieter over there at the bar by the fireplace," I touched her arm. "I'm all for dancing, but I'd also like to talk."

"Me, too." Elana nodded.

We found two seats at the quiet side of the bar. After being on my feet all day, it felt good to sit. I sat back in the high chair and swung my feet like a kid since they couldn't reach the floor. When the bartender asked, I ordered a hot toddy, hoping it would warm me up.

Elana slunk down in the seat and let out a happy, relaxed sigh.

"It's good to be here again with you. Like the old days."

"You mean, like two months ago," I raised an eyebrow at her.

Elana laughed and turned red, a little embarrassed. "Yeah. Well, I've missed you, so it feels a lot longer than that."

"I know what you mean. So many things I wanted to text you or call you about."

"I'm so glad we met up at the rental, Gracie." Then she lowered her voice. "Anything new on Daniel's case?"

It helped me to do some external processing, and Elana was a great person to bounce ideas off of. "We found out Daniel was blackmailing someone—Marco, the bakery reviewer from the class. He was at your table."

Elana brightened. "I remember him. He came in late."

I told her about my phone conversation with Marco/Mark's sister. "He lied about his education and experience. Daniel found out and used it to blackmail him."

Elana shook her head. "Why, though? Daniel had a successful business. I wouldn't think he'd need the money."

I nodded. "Daniel was not a nice guy. He enjoyed using people, so it's not surprising he'd use this guy for what he could get from him. I don't think he blackmailed him for the money—he wanted to get publicity and glowing reviews from this guy."

"If that's the case," Elana said, picking up a handful of

pretzels from the bowl on the bar. "Maybe the reviewer got sick of Daniel manipulating him. He'd have to drop everything and do Daniel's PR for him whenever he wanted it."

The bartender set my hot toddy down in front of me. I took a sip and felt the warmth seep through my whole body. Elana took a gulp of her cosmopolitan.

"But the reviewer's not the only suspect. And Rafal, the baker Daniel fired—he isn't really off the hook, or at least the Chief doesn't think so. He admitted to us that he wanted to hurt Daniel after he was fired."

"What about the wife?"

I told her my observations about how Ashley Fontaine was handling her new duties at Night Rose. "She doesn't seem to have any intention of selling the place, and she's in over her head running it. But she's still a suspect; she was with Daniel the whole time in River Grove."

Elana thought for a bit as she finished off a pretzel. "Who else spent a lot of time around Daniel recently?"

"Well, with the timing of the poisoning—Ashley, Omar, and anyone at the class, which would include Marco."

As I pictured the class attendees in my mind, a thought stuck in my head—just out of reach of me putting it to words. Maybe I'd overheard it in conversation during the class at the Laughing Loaf. I'd mentally written a note to myself to remember it. After class when Ashley had pounded on the door that Daniel had died, I'd lost the thought completely. Was what I heard related to Marco? Or someone else?

Shortly after we finished our drinks, the opening band finished its last song.

I felt my phone vibrate in my purse. I pulled it out to see the Chief was calling. There was no way I'd hear him in the noise of The Riverside.

"Elana, I'm going outside to take this call from the Chief."

"Don't stay out there too long, girl. The band will be on in a few minutes," Elana said distractedly, as she watched the roadies setting up for the headlining band. "Remember, we came here to *dance*."

"Yes, ma'am," I said with an exaggerated salute, as I got up and made my way to the front entrance. "The Chief doesn't call often, so I'm curious."

I was moving against the crowd, people streaming through the front doors, trying to find a table or a space on the dance floor.

Outside the entrance, on the wide, covered entry, it was much quieter. I clicked to answer the Chief's call.

"Dave, what's up?"

The Chief grunted. "I wanted you to know I met with Marco today. Gracie, it was not what I expected. He was very up front. He brought in bank statements showing a few payments he made to Daniel Bordleman. Daniel had been blackmailing him, but mostly to get him to give Night Rose video reviews and publicity. Marco told me it was ruining his channel—whatever that is—since he was running way too many episodes on the bakery. Marco decided he wanted to confess to his followers that he lied about his experience. The guy actually seems to feel bad that he'd lied."

"He chose a better way out of that situation," I said with a sigh of relief. "I'm glad."

"He decided it was cheaper to hire a public relations firm and tell Daniel to shove it, basically. Marco showed me their plan to rehabilitate his image—as he called it. He's going to volunteer to work for free in local restaurants and donate money to some culinary workers' aid fund."

I heard the Chief call out to someone in the background. "Gracie, Chloe's mother just came in from LA, so I should get going. But I wanted you to know."

I waited outside for a few minutes in the brisk night air before I went inside to the loud concert hall. We were back to the same suspects. At least there was one name crossed off the list.

I looked over the heads of the growing crowd to find Elana. In the short time I'd been outside, the noise level in The Riverside had ramped up. People were crowded around the bar, and the open floor space was packed. I stepped up into the high bar chair next to Elana.

"What did he say?" Elana leaned my way so we could hear each other.

"The reviewer didn't do it. He decided to come clean and confess he lied about his experience. He gave the Chief his bank statement showing payments and the papers, proving he'd hired a PR firm."

"Good for him." Elana said, glancing over at the stage with excitement. "Hey, it's almost time."

The drummer launched into the groove of the band's first song, and the bass started to twang. Elana slid off her seat, reached for my arm, and pulled me out toward the dance floor, which was already packed with music fans.

"C'mon," she said excitedly, her eyes gleaming. "Let's move up toward the front. I see an open spot near the stage."

We made our way through the crowd and found an area barely big enough for the two of us to dance, right below one of the speakers. The bass player was four feet away from us, and the loud deep bass notes reverberated through my body.

There was some freedom in that we were so squished up against the stage; no one could see us but the band.

Elana closed her eyes and went into her own world, swirling in a shiny silver skirt as she moved to the funk groove. I felt a pang of grief, remembering the last time I'd danced with Nate, outside the restaurant in Sonoma. I'd felt graceful and at ease. I would not feel this way on the floor of The Riverside tonight. I mean, I liked the idea of dancing. Elana got out there and danced with abandon. That was not me. I thought about it too much.

I finally gave up any ideas of doing it "right," and started enjoying myself. We danced through four songs before we looked at each other, and I shouted that my ears were starting to hurt. Elana shrugged and shook her head at me and shouted something back, but I couldn't understand a word she was saying. I waved in the direction of the bar, and we headed back to our seats, which Drake, the bartender, had saved for us.

I jumped up into the high seat with relief. "I forgot how noisy concerts are," I said, a little too loudly, my ears ringing.

"I'm surprised Reggie doesn't have serious hearing loss being here every night," Elana said, looking up and down the bar to see any newcomers, out of the mix of River Grovians and out-of-towners. She broke into a smile. "Wait a minute—isn't that bandana man? I still say he's good looking, but that bandana ruins the look."

I looked down at the lanky man standing at the end of the bar ordering. He was wearing his linen shirt, jeans and a bright goldenrod-colored bandana over his sandy blond hair. River Grove did have its share of 21st century hippies, but the man looked out of place in this crowd.

"Koa Wilson. He must still be staying with his dad in Santa Cruz," I said. "I'm surprised he's still in town. You'd think he'd need to be back in Eureka at his bakery."

"Let's go talk to him," Elana said, keeping her eyes on the man.

"I don't want to go talk to him," I sighed. "Can't we just enjoy ourselves?"

"Let's invite him over here, then." To my horror, Elana waved the tall man over.

The bartender reached across to hand him what looked like a tequila sunrise. Koa didn't look happy about Elana's invitation, but he moved down the bar to our seats.

"I'm surprised you're still in the area, Koa," I said with a friendly nod. "Still at your dad's?"

"Yeah." Koa looked around uneasily and took a seat next to me that had just opened up. He pulled out his phone and checked it. "He needed my help with the yard and some repair work on the house."

"You can be away from Moonbeams that long?"

He nodded hastily. "My staff's taking care of things while I'm away. It's good to give them some time to run things on their own."

"I get that," I took a quick sip of the hot Irish Coffee the bartender had just brought me. "Two weeks ago, I left my assistant manager Beck in charge of The Laughing Loaf, and she did a great job without me."

Elana leaned over the bar to connect with Koa's eyes. I'd realized back in October, when the Russians were stalking me, how good Elana was at this—schmoozing and getting info out of people. She smiled sadly and she leaned on one elbow. "So awful about Daniel, isn't it? Did you hear anything more about how he died?"

Koa's mouth twitched. He spoke calmly but there was anger in his eyes. Not sure if it was directed at us or the mention of Daniel. "He wasn't looking well at our class. I thought he was sick. Must have been something a lot worse, I guess."

The guy did not look comfortable with the conversation. He took a gulp of his tequila sunrise.

"Who knows?" Elana said with long heavy sigh. "I just hope they figure out what happened. Daniel was such a great baker. It's a big loss to the baking world." She shook her head dramatically and looked down into her drink.

Koa's face turned red. An angry red. He looked down at his phone.

"I'm sorry, ladies. I have an appointment to meet someone now. It's been good talking to you."

He set his half-full glass on the bar then turned and hurried for the front entrance of The Riverside.

Elana turned to me and smiled. "Wow, what was that about?"

"Just a sec. I'll be back." I stood up and watched Koa yank open The Riverside's heavy wooden door. Then I hurried to the front of the saloon and followed him out.

I stood at the edge of the parking lot, behind a big SUV, watching him wander through the lot, searching.

Near the last row of the parking lot, a car flashed its lights. Koa walked quickly along the row of spots until he got to a familiar silver Lexus. He pulled open the passenger door and slid inside.

As the parking lot lights shone down on the car, I was able to see through the windshield.

There was a young blonde woman at the wheel.

Ashley Fontaine.

Chapter Twenty

*M*onday, December 16

Elana buzzed about the conversation with Koa all the way back to my house, where Mary Jo's orange VW bug was still parked on the street in front of our house.

It was 10:45 p.m.

Seriously, you two. I heaved a sigh of irritation.

"Maybe Koa and Ashley were in it together," Elana said as she pulled into our driveway. "I can see Ashley, maybe. But why Koa? He didn't work for Daniel, and he doesn't even live in the area."

I tried to think of possible explanations for this. It was very odd that Ashley, who was supposed to be running Night Rose up in Sonoma County, had come back to River Grove, more than two hours away.

Maybe the Chief had asked her to come down for another interview? Judging by her behavior at Night Rose yesterday, she would have put up a fight about that.

Then I thought of something—what if Koa had moved in on Ashley after Daniel's death, romanced the grieving widow—knowing she'd be the new owner of the famous bakery? If he was still at his dad's in Santa Cruz, she could have come down here to meet with him.

"If Koa was seeing Ashley—" I tried to think this through as I said it out loud, "that could be a motive right there. Get rid of Daniel. *Boom!* You have a really profitable bakery."

Connections formed in my mind. I remembered Daniel's look of disgust as Koa approached him after class. I turned to Elana.

"Do you have some time? Would you come with me to the bakery so I can check something out?" I smiled. "I don't feel like going into my house right now."

Elana looked at the orange VW then shot a knowing look at me. "Mary Jo's still there? Things must be heating up. Should I really be aiding you in running from your dad's girlfriend?" She thought for a moment then started her car. "The Laughing Loaf it is."

Downtown was dark, except for The Riverside, which was still pumping funk bass lines and drum beats out into the starry darkness. We passed shops and City Hall, all lit by their outside lights. The counter lights and dining area pendant lights were on dim at The Laughing Loaf, so the bakery had a nice warm glow as we passed it to turn into the alley. Elana crunched over the gravel and parked next to the back entrance.

I turned the key in the back door lock, and we went inside, shivering in the cold night. I flipped on all the lights and headed for my tiny closet of an office. I turned on my really old PC and waited. Elana pulled up a chair next to mine.

"This is the Zoom session I had with Daniel that week before the class." After the whir of an ancient fan that was trying really hard, the computer finally displayed the login screen. I entered my password, then logged into Zoom. "At that point, I was getting that Daniel was a picky guy. I wanted to make sure I had his instructions for prepping for the class."

I clicked to bring up the video recording of our conversation. There was Daniel, looking tired—and in the light of what I now knew—maybe a little pink. He was complaining that I should have asked him specifically what brand of flour and gluten percentage to order for the sourdough class. I think what I'd seen came near the end of our talk. I forwarded the recording.

Since I'd chosen to display a transcript of our conversation, subtitles of our words appeared on the screen:

THIS IS GOING TO TAKE YOUR TINY BAKERY IN THE STICKS AND PUT IT ON THE MAP

Now I remembered what had stuck in my head about our conversation.

Daniel and I were near the end of our call when I saw a flash of color to the side of the screen.

Elana leaned toward the computer and cried out. "Stop! Did you see that?"

I stopped and went back a few seconds in the recording, then hit play. I knew what it was as soon as I saw it, and I hit pause.

"The bandana. It's the red one Koa wore at class," Elana said excitedly. "And I see part of his silver ear cuff."

Somebody off camera grunted out some words. I couldn't make it out. The program's transcriber tool was having a hard time deciphering it, too.

The caption appeared on the screen:

YOU WILL BAY FOR WATCH
YOU DITTO MEAT!

"What?" Elana snorted with laughter as she read the captioning. "What is that supposed to mean?"

"I guess it could be, 'You will pay for what you did to me.'" I rolled my chair back from my desk. "The voice recognition software isn't always the best."

I was puzzled. What had Daniel done to Koa? I didn't think they'd known each other before the woodfired class. No looks of recognition. But after our sourdough class, Daniel had turned Koa away with a look of disgust.

"Let's think about this, Elana," I swiveled toward her in my chair. I rubbed my eyes. It was 11:15 p.m. and I had to get up in five hours. "We've got three people who are connected to each other in some way—Koa Wilson, Daniel Bordleman, and Ashley Fontaine. I have a feeling Koa knew Daniel before the woodfired class at Night Rose. In fact, I remember when we were waiting outside for the class at Night Rose, Koa said—*believe me, he's a hothead.*"

"Maybe they'd gotten to know each other at some baking event?" Elana flipped open the top of her water bottle and took a drink. "They both seem like the alpha male type. Maybe they had a bad interaction there."

"Yeah, but remember Koa's reaction at the bar when you talked about Daniel?"

"He was angry. Very angry," Elana nodded.

I wondered where Koa had been during those weeks between the woodfired class at Night Rose and the sourdough class at The Laughing Loaf. He could have been hard at work at Moonbeams in Eureka—at least until he came down for the sourdough class.

Or maybe he'd gone up to see Ashley in Sonoma.

I already knew: Ashley had constant access to Daniel. She'd worked with him, stayed with him at the rental. She was there from the video filming through the class at Laughing Loaf. She had the most access to him of anyone.

IF I WANTED to find out where Koa had been during that time period, maybe I should call his bakery and ask his staff. I didn't have the time to drive up to Eureka, but I did have some ways to find information.

"I want to find out a few things about Koa," I said, through a yawn. "When I get a break tomorrow, I'll work on that."

Elana looked at me with concern. "Girl, you need to get some sleep if the bakery's going to open tomorrow. Let me take you home."

I locked up and Elana started up the car.

When we pulled into our driveway, the orange VW was no longer in front of the house.

I LOCKED THE FRONT DOOR, turned off the kitchen light, and went directly to my room, where Biga lay curled up on the bed waiting for me. He raised his head, then went back to sleep.

I was tempted to sleep in my clothes, but instead I slipped into a big old Seahawks t-shirt. I set my alarm for way too early and got into bed.

When I plugged my phone into my charger on the nightstand, a notification popped up.

It was a text Nate had sent earlier. His first message since he'd left eight days ago.

Time stamp: Exactly 9 p.m.

A picture of a tiny owl, with soulful golden eyes under heavy feathery brows.

A Northern Pygmy Owl He's missing someone tonight.

I texted back a heart.

When I fell asleep, I'm sure it was with a smile on my face.

Chapter Twenty-One

Tuesday, December 17

The next morning, I woke with Nate's owl message lingering pleasantly in my mind.

I left Biga at home with my dad. I had things to do, and much as I loved my little dog, he would make things more difficult.

I texted the Chief that I'd like to meet with him this morning.

I slid my copy of *Night of the Living Bread* and a raincoat in my backpack in case the rain restarted today. By the time I was ready to leave, my father had come out of his bedroom and was sitting in his t-shirt and pajama bottoms and his worn and frayed bathrobe, at the kitchen table, sipping a cup of tea.

"You got home late last night." He said looking up at me soberly. "Later than you said you'd be."

I hadn't thought he'd notice, being with Mary Jo and all.

"Elana and I went back to The Laughing Loaf to do a little research." I gave him a quick summary of what had happened at The Riverside. He listened soberly and nodded. "I should have let you know, Dad. I thought—you were with Mary Jo, and I didn't think you'd notice."

He took a sip of tea and looked at me over the top of the mug. "You don't like her. She thinks you're avoiding her."

Dad, I do not have time for this today. Then an overwhelming feeling of guilt came back to me.

I was too tired to make up a response. "I guess I am. I am sorry. I know she's not a bad person. She's just not mom."

"What an overwhelming endorsement," he said, almost under his breath. "I happen to care about Mary Jo a great deal."

I felt my chest tighten. I didn't want to try to deal with this, while a list of everything I wanted to get done today scrolled through my brain, on electronic readout.

"I'm so sorry. I want to like her. I know she's important to you. It's been a long time...since mom. It's just hard to get used to someone new in our lives."

My father gave me a cold stare.

"Nate is someone new in our lives. I haven't had a problem getting used to him."

He was right. I had to be the one to step forward here. I had not taken this relationship seriously. I'd been waiting for it to run itself out.

"I want to get together with Mary Jo," I said, my voice wavering. "I do want to get to know her. Maybe just her and me. Would she do that?"

My father smiled faintly. "I'm sure she would."

* * *

BECK CAME through the back door of The Laughing Loaf about five minutes after I did, basket of fresh eggs from her chickens in her hand. After my dad's words, I wasn't in the mood for cheerful talk, so I cranked up a playlist of 80s electronic pop and got to work. She smiled and took out the beignet dough from the fridge.

After some feedback from customers, I'd tweaked my Mediterranean scones a little more. Mayor C had said she'd be happier if the dill were toned down, so I'd added some oregano and cut back on dill. I preheated the oven and pulled the first tray out of the freezer to bake.

"I need to talk to the Chief at 10:30, Beck. Can you handle things for about an hour?"

"Of course, Gracie." She looked over at me as she rolled out beignet dough. "Everything okay?"

"Nothing serious. I have a few things I have to take care of. And—a lot on my mind." I nodded. "Thanks for being willing to cover."

Beck smiled over at me. "It's no problem. Take as long as you want. After the pastry fest, I feel like I can handle almost anything."

A half hour before opening, I took out the number I'd written down from the Moonbeams website. I had Koa's mobile number, but I wanted to find out about his whereabouts from his employees.

I'd do a quick call and ask about Koa. Casually inquire about when he might be back at the bakery and maybe, how long he'd been away.

I punched in the numbers on my phone. Soon I received a series of discordant beeps and a message.

This number has been disconnected.

Moonbeams had either closed or its website had been set up to give the impression that Koa was up in the far reaches of Northern California baking bread.

When he was actually in Sonoma. And River Grove.

. . .

THE HIGH SCHOOLERS came in at 7 a.m. – loud and energetic. Their laughter and jibes at each other felt normal and reassuring. I tried to set aside my thoughts about Koa. I slid into a good-natured routine, serving food, handing out coffee and making conversation with the teens. I cleaned up at least one coffee spill.

Chloe Westerman came in looking cheerful and rested, with something wrapped in tinfoil. "Gracie! Good morning. I made my cinnamon rolls last night." She beamed. "I brought you and Beck each one. My mom tasted them after she got back last night and said she loved them." She handed me the foil bundle.

I held it up to my nose and inhaled the cinnamon-caramel aroma. "They smell amazing. Thanks. I'll make sure Beck gets one."

When the customer line died down at 10:30 a.m., I made myself a good strong latte with two-percent milk. I took the notes I'd typed up and went across the street to talk to the Chief at City Hall.

Peony Roberts, her hair piled high on top of her head, looked me over skeptically as I came in, as usual.

"Gracie Markley. And who are you here to see?" Who did she think I was here to see?

"I have some important information for the Chief."

As she picked up her phone to call the Chief's office, I preempted her by running down the hall. After all, the Chief knew I was coming.

I poked my head into the Chief's office, then went in and set the latte down on his desk.

The Chief brightened and reached for it eagerly. "Thank you, Gracie. Sit down. I want to make sure I understand everything that happened last night at The Riverside. I've also got the crime scene report this morning. They managed to rush it."

My heart sped up as I pulled up a chair. "Tell me about the report."

"Good news is, no traces of cyanide inside The Laughing Loaf," he said, looking at me. "But in the trash can between the bakery and the old Antiques Emporium, they found a discarded plastic RG's Pizza El Biggo Drink cup with liquid in it. More than enough cyanide in it to make someone very sick. Or to finish someone off." He shook his head. "But no prints on it."

I told him about what the Zoom recording had shown—and what Koa had mumbled to Daniel from off camera. And how angry Koa had gotten when Elana talked about Daniel last night. Then he'd gotten into the car with Ashley.

"It was definitely her car, and she was driving," I said. "It was odd because apart from the class on Saturday, I didn't think the two knew each other."

The Chief took a gulp of his latte and leaned back in his seat, his hands folded across his belly. "From what you're telling me, Gracie, Koa Wilson and Daniel Bordleman knew each other before. I'd bet on it. I'm just not sure how or from where."

"I called Koa's supposed bakery in Eureka—Moonbeams. Its number's disconnected. Koa told me last night that he was able to be away from the bakery so long because he trusted his staff to take over for him. He could have been anywhere during the past few weeks."

"Do you have an address for Koa Wilson? I'll bring him in for questioning today," the Chief said.

"He said something about his dad living off of West Cliff in Santa Cruz. But I don't have any address."

I went back across the street, dodging falling rain, to relieve Beck. At 11:15 a.m., there was no line at the bakery, and the dining area tables were filled with people quietly reading or working on their laptops, while slowly savoring their coffee and tea.

I went behind the counter to check in with Beck. "Looks pretty quiet. No sudden rush?"

Beck shook her head as she wiped down the espresso machine. "Everyone's just chilling, happy to be out of the rain."

After prepping the dough for tomorrow's bread bakes, I went to my backpack and pulled out *Night of the Living Bread*. I sat at a table in the dining area and leafed through the pages. I skimmed through Daniel's story, in which he proudly declared he was the "one who was right." In his words, he'd had the vision that his former partner at his previous bakery didn't have.

But what bakery had that been? I wanted to know the story.

There were still shots of Daniel from his videos, marveling at risen dough, in his Frankenstein monster costume. Peering excitedly through an oven window at the golden dome of a boule of bread as it baked. A shot of a beautifully scored loaf of bread with a wreath of vines and leaves circling it. Daniel, knife in hand, instructing a table of Night Rose bakers on the proper way to chop herbs. Rafal must have loved that.

As I was flipping through the book, I saw a photo of Daniel in a baking room that did not look like Night Rose. It was much smaller and there were no woodfired ovens. I scanned the photo for clues as to where this bakery could be. I finally saw a stack of bread bags lying on a table. I enlarged the photo and peered closer at the bags.

I could make out a name: A Better Loaf

Excited, I went to my computer and looked up A Better Loaf.

The first listing was for Yelp. **A Better Loaf – Carmel, California — CLOSED 2016**

I scanned through the photos posted. They showed beautifully browned loaves, baguettes, batards, boules, muffins and scones.

Then standing in front of A Better Loaf's shop window, Daniel Bordleman and Koa Wilson, shaking hands and smiling.

Chapter Twenty-Two

I took a deep breath.

Not an exaggeration that I ran into the back room to my computer and began googling A Better Loaf.

I got a list of news articles, some from the town's local newspaper *The Carmel Pine Cone*, and a few in the San Jose Mercury News.

What happened to A Better Loaf: *Financial Mismanagement, Partner Claims*

A Better Loaf Closes after Two Short Years

Good Bread, Bad Blood: Carmel's A Better Loaf Closes

Daniel and Koa's partnership in the bakery, set in the quaint town of Carmel south of Santa Cruz, had ended in financial disaster. In the articles, Daniel claimed that Koa didn't have the baking background to run A Better Loaf.

Koa claimed that Daniel spent money recklessly and made all decisions without consulting him. In interviews, Koa said he'd had to pay more than his share of the debts after the bakery folded. He'd been left with loans to pay back after the bakery closure, while Daniel had gotten off the hook.

I went back to Yelp and looked up Koa's Moonbeams bakery in Eureka. The bakery had been closed, permanently, since October.

I printed out several of the articles to take across the street to the Chief. I texted him that I was heading over with some info.

He had to bring Koa in today.

Then I texted Elana what I'd learned and told her I was going to the Chief.

"Gracie, I'm taking off now," Beck washed her hands at the sink and went to get her coat and basket. "Everything's set for tomorrow morning. I rolled out extra beignet dough for peppermint chocolate beignets, since it's getting close to Christmas and people have been asking for them."

I turned from the computer screen and smiled. "Perfect. I have to go see the Chief, then I'll be back to shape loaves and finish up. See you tomorrow, Beck."

I slid the printouts into a folder. I pulled on my raincoat, slipping my phone into my front breast pocket. I locked the front door and looked both ways at the curb to cross the street. The wind was whipping up today, the first signs of a coastal storm brewing.

A familiar silver car screeched to the curb in front of me.

Before I knew it, strong arms had wrapped around my chest, pressing my arms to my sides.

A door opened, and I was shoved into the back seat.

Chapter Twenty-Three

I almost tumbled to the floor as Ashley Fontaine hit the gas pedal, and we sped away from downtown, heading for the coast.

Koa sat uncomfortably close to me, smelling more like sweat than fresh laundry today. He took out a roll of packing tape, peeled off a strip with his teeth, and wrapped it around my hands twice. As I moved my hands, I felt the tape pulling hairs out of my skin.

Koa opened the folder I'd been carrying and leafed through the printouts.

"You've got it all right here. The story of what Daniel did to ruin my life. I was left with nothing but bills to pay after A Better Loaf went out of business."

Not knowing what Koa was planning to do with me, I decided to take a sympathetic approach.

"I read it. Daniel treated you badly, used you. He ran A Better Loaf into the ground. Then he went on to start Night Rose, while you had to close Moonbeams."

Koa spoke in a choked voice. "All because of his bad decisions. I couldn't get financing for Moonbeams, so I tried to get by with my savings. I did okay for a few years, until we had some issues with the old building and couldn't afford to fix them. In August, I approached Daniel for a loan, and he said no. He laughed at me."

Ashley spoke from the front seat, "Hon, he only cared for himself. He deserved what he got."

I'd suspected this. Ashley was now on Team Koa.

Koa continued, his voice raspy. "He deserved a slow, painful death. That's exactly what he got."

Again, I tried to sound sympathetic. "I can see that you'd be angry after all he did to you, Koa."

Ashley responded to me, as we sped down Highway 17. "Koa bought the cyanide from some foreign seller on the internet. It's a pesticide. They don't even sell it in the U.S."

"I tested it out on Daniel with smaller doses, usually in drinks. He got tired and weak. And pinker," she added with a soft laugh. She gave a quick loving look back at Koa. "We both thought it was best to finish him off down here in River Grove. You know, keep the bad press away from Night Rose."

Nice. Leave me and The Laughing Loaf with the bad publicity.

"So...you two are a couple?" I was now mad at them both, but I tried to ask it as casually as I could.

"Since September," Ashley said warmly. "I started to see what a bad person Daniel was. How he used people. I was blind to that for so long. But Koa started calling me, asking me how the bakery was doing. He is such a good listener. We became friends. And then—more." She shot another loving look back at Koa.

I flinched as the car swerved into the next lane.

"I saw what a good heart he has. Koa really loves me. Daniel just used me."

You are still being used, Ashley. Then I looked at Ashley's innocent, smiling face in the rear-view mirror and felt a little guilty. After my experience in Seattle, who was I to judge?

I heard Koa's voice, warm and affectionate. "I can help you with the bakery, Ash. We will run Night Rose together. I'll teach you, not just make all the decisions myself like Daniel did."

It all made sense. Daniel had shafted his bakery partner in Carmel, big time. Now Koa had moved in to flip the scenario. He'd taken Daniel's wife and his popular and profitable bakery. It was wrong, but to Koa it was perfectly justified. A debt paid off.

Ashley was easy prey for Koa. She realized how much Daniel had used her, though of course, she was unable to see how Koa was playing her like a pawn in his scheme to take over Night Rose.

Ashley pulled into the exit lane for the Santa Cruz Municipal Wharf. I tried to imagine—why here? But I knew this was not going to end well.

With the storm about to hit the Bay Area, there was a high surf warning, not the best time to hang out on the coast. King tides were predicted—huge, surging waves that were becoming more and more common along the California coast.

Koa looked out at the moody sky, full of heavy grey clouds. It was 4 p.m.. Between the clouds and the waning daylight, it was getting dark and very cold.

"Perfect day to go to the beach," Koa said, looking cheerfully at the big waves crashing on the sand. As we neared the wharf, there were crowds of people on the beach, but most of them stood at a safe distance, wary of the strong surf.

Ashley drove onto the long pier, which had parking spots near the fishing spots, shops and restaurants. The car jolted as it rolled over the uneven asphalt surface. I moved my hands in my packing tape cuff, trying to create some wiggle room. My skin burned from the pull of the strong adhesive.

There were few people on the pier today and most seemed to be hurrying to their cars or down the pier in the direction of the shore. Waves crashed up against the sides of the pier. Each wave seemed to rise higher, splashing spectacularly up onto the deck.

Ashley parked in a spot behind a seafood store and café that I'd been to before with Elana.

I was curious as to why we were here. I was pretty sure it wasn't for fish and chips.

Ashley turned around in her seat and looked at Koa. She looked nervous, as if she might have doubts about what they were about to do. She paused, not ready to get out of the car.

"Ashley, get out now. We need to do this fast and get out of here. I'll take care of her."

Koa got out of the car first, and then grabbed me by an arm and pulled me up out of the car. I felt unstable on my feet and couldn't use my hands to steady myself. I slammed into the car door.

If I could somehow reach my phone, I could set off the SOS, which would notify emergency services of my location and that I was in danger. With my hands tied, there was no good way to do this. As I tried to right myself, I pressed my arms up against my chest where my phone was stashed in my breast pocket and squeezed them together. It was a lame attempt to try to activate the alert, and it only drew attention to me.

As she came around to our side of the car, Ashley looked at me suspiciously.

"She's got something in her coat, hon. Let's check."

Koa patted me down, then found the pocket and unbuttoned it. He pulled out the cell phone, and turned back to me, looking like a disappointed parent.

"You were hiding this. It's not going to do you any good." With that, he walked over to the pier railing and tossed my phone into the ocean. A wave rose up onto the deck right after that, as if the sacrifice had been accepted.

"I thought you were more sympathetic, Gracie. It looks like we can't trust you." He reached into his pocket and pulled out a small, black pistol. "I hope you understand, Gracie," he said in a soft, earnest voice. "How much I hate having to use this. I am not a man of violence."

He's going to shoot me. On this pier—which everyone seems to be evacuating.

I looked around for any possible path to safety. Chances were, if I ran, it would only make it easier for him to shoot me. There was no one around to cry out to. The end of the pier looked deserted.

Ashley came up behind him, touching his arm gently and pleading in a soft voice.

"No, Koa. Don't shoot her. Give her a chance at least. Make her jump."

Koa sighed with exasperation. "Fine." He pointed the gun at my back and forced me to the railing. "Climb up, Gracie."

I put a foot on the railing fence, then stepped up. I felt the gun barrel at the small of my back. Then I jumped off the fence, seeing the churning water below me come closer.

Then smack. I was in.

Chapter Twenty-Four

I was deep in an icy cold, constantly shifting mass.

Kelp grabbed at my ankles. Something nibbled at my arm. My head spun dizzily as the ocean seemed to shove me back and forth like a ping pong ball.

I pulled at my wrists and as soon as my head broke through the surface, I gasped for air. A wave knocked me against a post of the pier, which was slimy and cold. I tried to feel for anything I could hold onto, but it was all slippery goo.

But as the slime coated my arms, it seemed easier to move my hands. and slowly, I pulled them out of the cuff of tape, which drifted away from me. Then I slipped down under, knocked by a wave. I sank but held my breath until I bobbed back to the surface.

If I kept next to the pier pilings, I reasoned, Koa and Ashley couldn't see me. I'm sure they were looking for me. I kept close to the pier, swimming now. The crashing waves pulled me back and forth, and I didn't feel like I was making much progress. Another wave smacked me hard against a piling.

Soon a strong wave gave me a ride and pushed me forward. The shore seemed a little closer now.

The memory came back to me, in such a strong way that my body even felt it. Swimming in cold Puget Sound, at summer camp on Vashon Island near Seattle. I remembered the drill I had to do if I wanted to use the canoes—I was dumped out of a canoe and had to make it back to shore on my own.

I struck out, swimming, till I realized that the waves were going to do what they wanted to do with me, and I had little choice. There were times when I let them carry me; other times I fought them. But gradually, the shore was coming closer.

I looked up and to my left. I was no longer close to the pilings, and I was sure it was a matter of time before Koa would spot me in the open and finish me off.

At this point, though, I had one goal.

I looked ahead of me and aimed myself at the shore.

When I saw red lights in the distance, I thought I was hallucinating. The cold and exertion and maybe lack of oxygen were getting to me. I was losing this fight.

Rows of people—or maybe posts?—were lined up ahead of me on the sand. A fire truck. Cars with red and blue flashing lights. A siren wail.

Only a few more yards. I slumped onto the sand.

I felt a blanket wrap around me. Voices.

"Gracie Markley, right?"

"Gracie!"

"We've got you, ma'am. You're okay."

I was lying down on a stretcher. Suddenly I felt warm. Safe. Lifted and carried by friendly people in uniforms who wanted to save my life, not end it.

The faces looking on, calling to me, came into focus.
The Chief. Elana and Kirk. Mayor C.
And Beck.

Chapter Twenty-Five

Tuesday, December 17

After my run-in with the king tides, Beck would get three more days of running The Laughing Loaf on her own.

The EMTs took me to the hospital, where the emergency room doctor said it looked like I'd badly bruised at least two ribs but had no fractures. She guaranteed I'd be sore as hell the next day.

As he drove me home, the Chief questioned me about what had happened that day—and the details I'd found out about Koa and Ashley.

"We finally found the video camera and recording," the Chief said with a satisfied smile. "From a search of Ashley's house. The video shows her handing Daniel the RG's El Biggo cup. The same one the crime scene team found in the trash can in front of the bakery."

Koa and Ashley were arrested at the entrance to the wharf after I got to shore. A man coming out of a restaurant on the wharf called 911, saying he'd seen a woman forced off the pier at gunpoint.

When Elana hadn't heard back from the text she'd sent me, she called the Chief. She knew I'd been planning to pass info about Koa onto him.

At my house, Nate stood in the driveway next to my dad, looking pale as a ghost. He'd just gotten back from Oregon and had biked to our house. My dad had just told him what happened to me.

For two days, I lay on our living room couch under multiple down comforters, being attended to by Nate, Elana, my Dad and Mary Jo. I couldn't get warm enough. Mary Jo brought me cups of tea and homemade chicken noodle soup.

Nate slept in my dad's recliner all night and made sure I had ice or a heating pad on my ribs. He even brought his extended versions of *The Lord of the Rings* movies to watch. He stayed up late with me to watch all eleven and a half hours of them. We both cried (and then fell asleep) at the end of *Return of the King*.

I wanted to get up and go to work at The Laughing Loaf, but I knew —I wouldn't be able to do that for a while.

"Gracie, I've got this," Beck reassured me when I called to tell her. "The only thing I'm not clear on is the bread. Can you coach me through that? Also, I'll need some help because it's a school day, and Chloe and Aiden can't be there till 3. I'm not quite sure who we can call. My mom might be able to come in."

I'd met Beck's mom, Denise, a few times. She was no-nonsense and scared me just a little, but I had eaten her baked goods, and they weren't bad.

But I had a better idea. I'd call someone who was between jobs.

Maeve Killoran excitedly said yes, she was available for the next three days and would drive down from Sonoma.

That next day, I experienced the benefits of living in a small town where everyone knew everyone's business.

News of my dangerous swim had gotten around. Janet from the Clip n' Curl brought me a chicken casserole, and Annie and Eric Morton brought a crock pot of his second-place, award-winning cookoff chili. Reggie McFerrin brought chips and a tub of his homemade guacamole, which he knew I loved. He stayed to play chess with my dad. He won two out of the three games they played.

Later that night, Chloe Westerman stopped by with her grandfather. She had a tray of warm cinnamon rolls, wrapped in foil. They smelled amazing. Nate and I split one.

"Gracie, I've been making them like I learned at The Laughing Loaf. They're really good, but my grandfather can't eat them now. It's probably not good to keep them around the house." The Chief put his arm around his grand-daughter and whispered thanks.

As December 25 approached, the weather in River Grove turned dry and very cold. I was back at the bakery again, and we were busy in preparation for the holidays.

One night, after dinner and a board game with my dad and Mary Jo, Nate and I put on our down jackets and scarves and escaped to the swing on the front porch. Dad and Mary Jo Hartman sat in the living room watching a rom com. It did not sound like a movie my father would want to watch in a million years. But, hey, relationships require compromise.

Biga was curled up in Nate's lap, asleep apparently, with his favorite person. Christmas lights and blow-up Santas and reindeer glowed in the front yards of the houses on our street. The very full river behind our house tumbled by, making soft sounds like whispered voices.

"Gracie, I need to talk to you about something."

Nate turned to me, a serious look on his face.

The tamales we'd eaten for dinner churned in my stomach. So this was the conversation we'd have about my witness protection status. But I didn't initiate it, like I'd had many opportunities to do in the car on the way to Sonoma and back. Or when we were cuddling together under a blanket at the "hut."

Instead, Nate was bringing it up, after his time in the great outdoors. I had no idea where this was going, and that scared me. *Damn.* Things had been going so well.

He smiled softly. He squeezed my hand.

"Will you come watch me play on the River Grove River Rats softball team this spring?" He watched my face as it went from fear to relief. "I'm first baseman."

My mouth felt stuck shut. I'd been preparing for a much harder question. I laughed nervously. "Mayor C got to you, didn't she?" I suddenly felt like crying.

"Corinne's very persuasive." He had a mischievous twinkle in his eyes. "I asked for a signing bonus, but she wasn't going for it."

"Of course not. She's a tough woman to bargain with." My lip trembled a little as I tried to smile. "I can't wait to see you play."

We sat quietly, in that companionable silence we usually had. We didn't talk for about five minutes, as we breathed the fresh, crisp air, and heard the distant sounds of my dad and Mary Jo laughing at the movie they were watching.

Nate reached for my hand again and squeezed it.

"Gracie, I've been doing some research." He looked at me significantly. "And I *know*."

"You've let a lot of things slip." There was a trace of a smile on his lips. "Maybe that was on purpose. When we were at the house in Sonoma, you said you went to Girl Scout camp on an island in the sound. That has to be Puget Sound in Seattle. Portland—where you said you grew up— doesn't have a sound."

I gulped and looked down at my hands, still unable to speak. "Okay. Yeah."

"You grew up in Seattle. It makes sense with other comments you've made." He pressed his lips together. "So I looked some things up. Two years ago, someone turned in a software engineer named Benjamin Morrison, who was selling defense secrets. There were rumors that his wife did it. And that her name was Grace. But after the trial, any mention of Grace Morrison disappeared. No government records. Nothing on social media. A reporter who'd written an article about the trial told me the only case where she'd seen this happen was when an informant who testified in court went into witness protection."

I closed my eyes. I couldn't breathe.

"So I decided to test this when you picked me up from the airport, after I came back from the Galapagos. I started calling you Grace." We looked out at strings of blue Christmas lights, which had just lit up the house across the street. "You looked terrified. I figured I was right."

My heart pounded so hard, I was sure he could hear it.

"It was the right thing to turn him in, but it took a lot of courage. He was selling dangerous secrets. He probably tried to bring you down with him, too. When we were on the trip, you said something that stuck with me: 'Sometimes the only reward for doing the right thing is knowing you did the right thing.'"

Nate looked at me, his eyes watery. "You lost everything. Your job, your friends and your marriage—though Ben makes Daniel Bordleman look like a saint, if you don't mind me saying so." He was doing the nostril flaring thing again, and the muscles in his face clenched. He was angry on my behalf. He studied my face. "It's true, isn't it?"

I nodded slowly.

"I've lost people in my life," he continued, his voice low and soft. "If I stayed with you, I could lose you, too. I don't know the details, but I think that almost happened in October, while I was doing the Galapagos shoot."

"It did." I said, almost whispering.

"I wanted to think about it—really make a decision. I want to keep everyone I care about safe. But that's not how things work. There are no guarantees. Losing someone is hard. I know you understand that."

I lay my head against his arm. He pulled me closer.

"I thought it would be easier for you if I said all this, because I know you--you keep the promises you make. Not everyone does that." He said it firmly. I felt a lump in my throat. After weeks of holding it back, I started to cry.

"Grace Kristen Hollis Morrison. *Gracie.*" Pressed up against him, I felt his deep voice as it rumbled in his chest. "I'm in. I'm not going anywhere."

THE END

Thank you

Thank you for reading
Sourdough and Cyanide!

If you enjoyed this book, please consider leaving a review or rating on Amazon, Goodreads or the book review site of your choice.

I truly value the time you take to do this, and it makes my author heart happy.

Also by Victoria Kazarian

Drop Dead Bread - Laughing Loaf Bakery Mystery #1

Bread to Rights - Laughing Loaf Bakery Mystery #2

Trouble You Don't Knead - Laughing Loaf Bakery Mystery #3

Stop, Drop and Rolls: A Laughing Loaf Bakery Short Mystery
(prequel novella)

Traditional mystery

writing as **VL Kazarian**

(Detectives Jimmy Ruiz and Dani Grasso):

Swift Horses Racing – Silicon Valley Murder Book 1

Across the Red Sky – Silicon Valley Murder Book 2

A Tree of Poison – Silicon Valley Murder Book 3

Acknowledgments

The writing process for this book was crazy, because my life in the last part of 2023 was exactly that.

In the five months of writing this book, I took two international trips with family, went to a week-long convention, and had two major illnesses, the second of which made me completely dependent on my husband and kids for two weeks. I'm so thankful to Pete, my husband, and to my children Armen and Lisa, for taking such good care of me. And for making sure I didn't try to get up and do things on my own, which would have made things worse.

This book came together in stops and starts. I'm thankful to everyone who encouraged me, talked plot with me, read it through to see if it made sense, and made me laugh, during the process. Thank you to Sisters in Crime for the write-ins that helped me catch up on my word count.

Thank you to my editor, Honest Magpie, who at times took my characters more seriously than I did—and especially felt that Gracie should be kinder to her father's girlfriend.

Thank you to my beta readers: Pam Milliken, Faye Friesen Myers, Kerry Nozicka, Chris Anderson, and Amanda Giles. Thank you for sticking with me through this series, giving me perspective on it, and finding misplaced words and awkward sentences. Thank you to Chris Anderson for her brilliant ability to see timeline issues and inconsistencies. And thank you to Mary Ann Askins, proofreader extraordinaire, for finding the errors and typos that I always seem to gloss over.

And gratitude to Debbie Cunningham, book evangelist, who keeps my books on her coffee table for guests. She's been known to visit bookstores on her world travels, asking:

"Do you carry my friend's books? You know—*you should.*"

About Victoria Kazarian

Victoria Kazarian lives and writes in San Jose, California. After working for years as a Silicon Valley marketing professional, she taught high school English and actually owned a bread bakery of her own called The Laughing Loaf. When she's not writing, she enjoys baking artisan breads and forcing her children and dog to go on road trips to the Pacific Northwest.

See what she's up to at victoriakazarian.com

You can contact Victoria—or perhaps leave a message for Gracie Markley herself—at TheLaughingLoaf@gmail.com

Are you in a book club?

Interested in reading any of The Laughing Loaf Bakery Mysteries with your book club? I'd love to appear at your book club online - and possibly in person, if you're in the San Francisco Bay Area.

Contact me at thelaughingloaf@gmail.com

Laughing Loaf Bakery Recipes

Seven-Day Sourdough Starter from Scratch
Sourdough Loaf
Sourdough Discard Chocolate Chip Cookies
Sourdough Discard Crackers
Mary Jo's Chicken Tetrazzini

Seven-Day Sourdough Starter

There are many ways to get starter for making sourdough bread.

You can order it from a place like King Arthur Flour (see kingarthurbaking.com). Local bread bakeries will often sell it cheaply if you ask. Or you can make it yourself.

It's not that hard! It's all about consistency. Discard and feed at roughly the same time each day, keep it at a consistent temperature (between 76 and 85 degrees is ideal), and in a week or two, you'll end up with starter for your own bread.

You'll need:

•Large jar or glass container (about quart size) with a lid. A Mason or Bell jar is ideal.

•½ cup of whole wheat flour (you can buy very small bags of whole wheat at most stores)

•About 4 cups all-purpose or bread flour

•Water

Follow this schedule to end up with about 1-1/2 cups of starter.

Day 1: Add ½ cup of whole wheat flour to your jar, then pour in ¼ cup of warm water. Mix it up till it's pasty and there are no dry spots. Let this sit in a warm (not hot) place for today and the next day. Now, nothing to do till Day 3.

Day 3: Take out ½ of the mixture in your jar and discard it. Now add ½ cup AP or bread flour and ¼ cup warm water to the mixture. Mix it well.

Day 4: Take out ½ of the mixture and discard it. Now add your ½ cup AP or bread flour and ¼ cup warm water and mix it well again. You should start to see bubbles on the surface the next day. If you don't, be patient. It will happen.

Day 5: Take out ½ of the mixture and discard it. Now add your ½ cup AP or bread flour and ¼ cup warm water and mix it well again. If you've been seeing bubbles in the mixture, you'll see more this next day. If you don't, look for a warmer place—maybe in your dishwasher after running it, or in an oven that's been turned on briefly then turned off.

Day 6: Take out ½ of the mixture and discard it. Now add your ½ cup AP or bread flour and ¼ cup warm water and mix it well again. If you've been seeing bubbles, you'll see even more. The mixture should be rising higher in the jar.

Day 7: Take out ½ of the mixture and discard it. Now add your ½ cup AP or bread flour and ¼ cup warm water and mix it well again. If you've been seeing a lot more tiny bubbles and the starter is rising higher and higher in the jar each day, you should be just about ready. I recommend doing one more discard and feeding a day after this, just to make sure.

If you haven't seen quick growth or very many bubbles, don't worry. Look for a warmer spot and stay consistent with discarding and feeding. It may take you two weeks, but you will get there. If you see a dark liquid floating on the top of the starter, no worries. It's just a byproduct of the yeast – called hooch. Pour it off and keep up the discarding and feeding.

Think it's ready? Do this test: Fill a bowl with water, then drop a spoonful of starter into it. If it floats, even for a little bit, it's ready.

Once your starter is ready, you can keep it in your fridge. Do the feed/discard thing once a week. If you forget a week or two, no worries.

When you want to use it, take it out of the fridge and keep it at room temperature. With one day of discarding and feeding, your starter should be ready to use again.

Sourdough Loaf

Makes one loaf.

Total time: About 16-18 hours. Most of this time will be a slow rise in your refrigerator, so don't be like me--make sure you clear out a spot for the bowl!

Total time before refrigerator rise: About 4 hours, 45 minutes

Best way to bake this is in a Dutch oven – an oven-safe pot with a lid, either enameled or cast iron. Make sure the pot/dutch oven is able to withstand 475 degrees.

You'll need:

1-2/3 cup warm water (plus, set aside 2 teaspoons for later)

½ cup of your ready-to-go, bubbly starter

3 cups bread or all-purpose flour (bread flour will give you a higher rise) + 2/3 cup whole wheat flour

1 tablespoon sea salt

1. Add the water to a large mixing bowl then mix in the starter so it dissolves. Add the bread and whole wheat flours and mix till combined. Cover with a towel and set in a

warm place for one hour. This is the *autolyze* stage–this time of rest will make the gluten in your dough more stretchable and will begin to break down the starch in the flour into sugar—which will feed the yeast and make it happy. Autolyze is preparation for making a higher-rising, tastier loaf of bread.

2. After the hour of autolyze, add the salt and 2 teaspoons of warm water over the top of the dough and knead it in, using your thumb and forefinger like pincers (if you can) to snip the dough into balls, then squish them back together. Do this "snipping" twice until the dough is blended. If it's getting sticky, get your fingers wet with warm water.

3. Stretch and fold time. Pull one side of the dough, stretch it over the rest of the dough, then press it down. Turn the bowl around 180 degrees, then do this again, pulling the dough, stretching it and pressing it down again. If your hands get sticky, get them wet with warm water. Pull off any dough on the sides and bottom of the bowl and fold it in during this process, dusting the bottom of the bowl with flour so dough doesn't stick. Pick the dough up and dust the bottom of the bowl with flour to keep dough from sticking. Now cover the dough and let it rest for one more hour. Repeat this stretching and folding process two more times. You will be doing this stretch/fold/turn sequence a total of **three times**, with an hour between each—for a total of three hours.

4. Once you've done those, you'll shape your loaf before it goes into the fridge. Lightly flour a clean, smooth surface. Carefully lift the dough out of the bowl, dust the top with flour, and set it on the surface. Now with one hand on either side of the dough, rotate it while pressing in on the sides and

pressing down slightly on it. You're forming it into a round boule, and the turning is tightening it up.

5. Now take the dough out and set it into a floured proofing basket or just a medium mixing bowl with a dish towel in it (sprinkle flour into it before setting in the dough). Now cover the bowl or basket with plastic stretch wrap and a dish towel. Set this in the fridge to proof for a cold rise for 12-18 hours. The results of this cold rise will be noticeable —both in the flavor and the rise of your baked loaf.

6. About 30-40 minutes before baking, set your open dutch oven or pot in the oven on the middle rack and preheat to 475 degrees. The pot will come to temperature along with the oven. When your oven is to temperature, carefully remove your dough from the chilled bowl, set it into the pot, and put on the lid.

7. Bake for 25 minutes at 475 degrees, then reduce the oven temperature to 450 degrees. Now take the lid off your pot, and let it bake for another 10-15 minutes at this lower temp or until the loaf is golden brown or slightly darker. Keep an eye on it because it will get dark fast.

8. Take the pot out of the oven, setting it carefully on your stove or other safe surface. Use a spatula to remove the bread and set it on a cooling rack.

9. Let the bread cool for at least an hour, then slice.

Sourdough Discard Chocolate Chip Cookies

A delicious way to use your sourdough starter discard. These cookies are not sour at all. The starter just enriches the flavor and gives the cookies a lovely, soft texture.

You'll need:

    1-1/2 cup all purpose flour
    1 teaspoon baking soda
    1 teaspoon salt
    ½ cup (one stick) of butter
    1 cup brown sugar
    ½ cup discarded starter
    2 large egg yolks
    3 teaspoons vanilla
    2/3 cup chocolate chips

Preheat oven to 350 degrees. Prepare baking sheets by lightly greasing them or laying down baking parchment.

Mix the butter and brown sugar together till well blended. Then add the egg yolks, starter discard, and vanilla. In another bowl mix together the flour, baking soda and salt.

Now stir the bowl of dry ingredients into the wet ingredients. Mix them until blended and there are no dry spots, but don't overbeat them. Then fold in the chocolate chips.

Scoop out dough (about 2 tbsp each) in balls on the sheet, giving them a few inches of space, because they tend to spread out.

Bake for 9-11 minutes or until the edges are very lightly golden.

Do NOT overbake. The cookies will continue to bake on the sheet when you take them out. Let the cookies cool on the sheet until they are firm, which should be about ten minutes.

Sourdough Discard Crackers

Easy to make—and a little too easy to eat.

You'll need:

¾ cup of starter discard

2 tablespoons butter, melted

¼ teaspoon sea salt

¼ teaspoon garlic powder

1-1/2 teaspoons Italian seasoning

Preheat oven to 325 degrees. Put melted butter, discard, garlic powder and Italian seasoning into a bowl and mix it up. Then spread a sheet of parchment (or if you have a SilPat baking mat, even better) out on a baking sheet. Spread the mixture over the parchment/SilPat in a thin layer – so it's evenly spread and you can't see through it. Sprinkle the top with the sea salt.

Bake for ten minutes, the remove it. Using a knife or pizza cutter, score across the spread out dough to create squares roughly around 1-1/2 inches.

Put tray back in the oven and bake for 20-40 minutes,

until the crackers are golden brown. Watch them so they don't get too dark. Take them out, let them cool. Separate them and enjoy.

Mary Jo's Chicken Tetrazzini

An old-school, cheesy comfort casserole that Gracie's dad has come to love.

This converts to a gluten-free dish easily—just use gluten-free pasta and use cornstarch instead of flour for the creamy sauce.

The dish has roots in a place not far from River Grove, California. When Italian opera star Luisa Tetrazzini came to sing in San Francisco in the early 1900s, the chef at the city's elegant Palace Hotel created the dish and named it after her.

You'll need:

1 package, cooked and drained, of spaghetti or fettuccini

1 cup of sliced button mushrooms

1 stick (1/2 cup of butter)

½ diced onion

2 ribs of celery, diced

3 cloves garlic, minced

¼ cup white wine

¼ cup of white flour (or cornstarch if you're making this gluten free)

2 cups milk

1 cup chicken broth + one chicken bouillon cube dissolved in it

(if you're using Better than Bouillon rather than broth, you can just dissolve 2 tsp B-than-B in 1 cup hot water)

¼ tsp paprika

Salt to taste

Dash of pepper

1 cup grated mozzarella

1/4 cup grated or shredded parmesan cheese

2 cups cooked, chopped chicken (rotisserie chicken works great)

¼ cup chopped parsley

In a large pot, melt half of the stick of butter and add chopped mushrooms, onion, and celery. Cook till slightly soft, then at the end, add the garlic for a minute or two, but don't let it brown. Add the wine, scraping at the bottom of the pot to get any residue (deglazing), then pour everything in the pot into a bowl and set aside.

On medium low heat, add the remaining half stick of butter to the same pot and melt, then sprinkle flour or cornstarch over it. Stir it together, then slowly add milk and the chicken broth mixture. Stir till it thickens into a sauce, whisking it to make it smooth, then add paprika, salt and pepper to taste, then take it off the heat.

Now add to this sauce the cooked vegetable mixture, ½ cup of the grated mozzarella, the parmesan, the chicken, and the cooked pasta. Stir together till everything is coated with sauce. Put it all into a casserole dish, then sprinkle the top with the remaining mozzarella and the chopped parsley.

Bake at 375 degrees for about 25 minutes.

Follow me!

If you're on Facebook, follow me at **Victoria Kazarian - author** for additional recipes and content I'll be posting about *The Laughing Loaf Bakery Mysteries*.

* * *

Sourdough and Cyanide Playlist

To enjoy singing along with the songs Gracie and Beck sing as they bake, listen to the *Sourdough and Cyanide* playlist on Spotify:

Sourdough and Cyanide playlist